S.H.E Emerged

The Manifestation of Me

Chalimar S. Ramey

Living With Intention
Self-Publishing Services

S.H.E Emerged: The Manifestation of Me
Copyright © 2021
By
Chalimar Ramey
Cover Art By: Jermayne Noseal and Asante Ramey

ISBN: 978-1-63790-160-1

DEDICATION

First and foremost, I want to thank God for his grace and favor. For being a loving reminder of all that I am and all that I am destined to be. For saving me. For knowing my name. There is no greater love than that which you give.

This book is dedicated to my children. My big luv and my baby luv. Asante you are the Ruth to my Naomi. You saved my life, a lifeboat when I was drowning in the sea of turmoil. Shakayla, my warrior with the heart of Esther. The glue that holds us all together and commands more from me than I ever knew I was capable of accomplishing. My Son-shine, Deion, my light in the darkness with the heart of David. Continue to slay giants. Taylor, the best thing I never knew I needed, my balm of Gilead that soothes my soul. Alaysia my bonus baby, a real-life lesson in walking in love. Thank you all for giving me a reason, for being my reasons. Thank you for unconditional love, forgiveness when I did not get it right and patience while I figured it out.

To my husband, my King, my lover, and my friend. Thank you. Thank you for being exactly who and what your name means "Who is like God". A living breathing embodiment of God's heart for me. Thank you for your patience, love, kindness, and persistence. For never giving up on me or us. Thank you for holding me in your arms, wiping my tears and unwavering faith in me. Thank you for your yes and the honor of being your wife. You are the one God kept for me.

To my parents, Daddy, you are my guy. Thank you for fighting, for surviving and winning!!! Mom I forgive you. I love you and God has not forgotten you.

My one and only sister by blood Ebony. The first human being to make my heart skip a beat.

Shakilah, thank you for a lifetime of love and sistership. Thank you for never leaving me behind.

My sisters and partners in ministry the Mighty 7.

Thank you all for pushing, pruning, and loving me through. Thank you for accountability. Even at my worst you saw only the best and accepted no less. I am so excited to be doing life with you all.

To every child born into chaos, trapped in the bowels of despair, and forged in the fire of neglect, the broken, overlooked, lost souls who just want to be whole and free. To everyone who has ever just needed someone. You matter, I believe you, I believe in you, I love you and most importantly God loves you too. You are worthy of the love you so desire.

In Loving Memory of Shakita, Geneva, Willie Mae and Betty Mae.

A Note To Readers

2019 was a year of new beginnings in different ways. I suffered the devastating loss of someone very near and dear to me. Meanwhile, I also took the first steps into my spiritual purpose and calling, one that has been spoken over my life since birth. I was excited and on fire for God! Like most infants in Christ, I wanted to run to my destiny. I saw myself as being a part of the change the church so desperately needed, against all odds. I was ready for the challenge; or so I thought. In the haze of my newfound zeal, I forgot one key ingredient, me.

Due to experiences in my formative years, I adopted the mantra of being my sister's keeper. At an early age, I promised myself that I would not only be a better person than who people had been to me, but also that I would be the person I needed. This came easy for me as I had developed a servant's heart at an early age. Love, validation, and belonging were things I craved so I gave them freely and worked overtime to secure those things from people around me even when it was not reciprocated or deserved. I would later learn those ideas were unhealthy for me. Non the less my ministry was built around these principles and values. Sisterhood, community, and togetherness. The village. These things were important to me and would become my core values.

I recognized early on that I could not be effective as a person, mother, wife nor would I really begin to live my best life if I did not address the things that I had buried down on the inside. As I matured in my spiritual walk, I also knew getting to the root of these things would be necessary for me to bear the fruits of and operate in the calling God had placed on my life. I thought I had spent the latter years of my life getting to the root of my traumas and freeing myself of the toxic characteristics that developed because of those traumas.

I quickly learned I was wrong. Forced to really sit with myself undistracted, brought about the realization that my childhood traumas and toxic past were still influencing my behavior. What I thought I had been addressing for years was not gone. I had become functional in it. I had simply suppressed it and God was about to force me back into the journey of healing.

With my ministry on its way and new divine connections developing, what could be wrong? What could go wrong? Well just as complicated as 2019 had started off was as complicated as it would end. Ushering me right into the shutdown of life as I had known it in 2020. My journey through 2020 was so needful and I can say with certainty that each experience was God ordained, including a few tricks of the enemy. What I would leave behind and walk into would lay the foundation and help me push through to my greatest manifestation, the manifestation of ME.

2020 would prove to be challenging on many levels. I faced a lot of challenges and suffered some losses. Most importantly I found myself at a crossroads. My usual distractions of trying to solve everyone else's problems was gone, and I was left to face ME. For the first time in my adult life, I was left with nothing but time on my hands and the eerie sound of my inner monolog. It was sobering to say the least.

The journey of healing and walking toward one's wholeness can be daunting. It is a process that will propel you into many highs, lows, peaks, and valleys. It takes courage and determination to not only revisit your traumas, but to also work through them. It's an ever-evolving process that takes years of consistent work and effort. Although most people feel that 2020 was a horrible year, for some like myself, it was a year of reflection and resolution. With the world shut down, we were forced to spend extensive amounts of time in our homes. I believe that God was commanding our attention and wanted us to truly take inventory of ourselves and get back to him without outside distractions.

Often, we get so busy and caught up in the routine of our lives that we forget to take time to focus on what should be the most important thing to us, that being self-care. As women this can sometimes be difficult. We maneuver careers, faith, family, marriage, and for some ministry. We tend to take on so much in our day to day lives and while we try to keep everyone around us afloat often, we find ourselves internally sinking sometimes even drowning.

Although my life in its entirety would probably make for a great novel all in its own, that is a story for another time. For now, let's focus on the "highlight" reel so to speak. These pivotal moments would not only define me, but they would also provide greater insight into just how easily toxic traits and traumatic experiences had weaved themselves into the very fiber of my being. These moments shaped not only my view of others but also how I viewed myself. So, grab your favorite beverage, snacks and some tissues and join me on my journey from trauma to triumph and see a true example of what it means to be saved by God's grace, healed by his stripes, and covered by his blood. This is my redemption song. This is how **S.H.E Emerged. S.H.E is Saved Healed and Enough. S.H.E. is ME!**

Foreword

This story opens like so many other stories that we have either been witness to or have lived ourselves. It takes not only a level of boldness to put such a story to paper for the world to read, but it also takes a level of healing to be able to stand in what is coming after the story goes to print. Many of us have shared our stories in small groups and occasionally across various platforms in part; but to open the different ventricles and layers of the heart we dare not allow others to see in to, that takes a huge step of faith and a level of Godly-confidence and trust that many are still finding their way towards.

When mothers and fathers are not well and whole enough to love and to sacrifice their all for the seeds they birth into the world, they leave a scar on a child's heart that is not easily healed. Our parents are our first nourishers, teachers, protectors, voices of reason and examples of what it means to love and be loved. When they do not show up in these ways in our lives, they leave us to ourselves, to our friends, to the world – which can all be very cruel and unkind places to the vulnerabilities of a child who is searching to know their identity, for acceptance and just to be loved. Then add to the lack of parenting, parenting or protection gone array at the hands of others. Why our families choose to stay silent amidst the boogieman in the dark, we may not ever understand. It is the shame, or some guilt for the lack of protection provided which leaves room for the nightmare to happen in the first place? The enemy of our souls loves this level of silence and this action of sweeping it all under the rug as if none of it ever happened. How damaging to the soul this is for anyone who has ever had to endure trauma to this level. The turmoil a heart goes through to try to understand what love really is when love refuses show up to rescue them. The lie a soul lives with, to constantly tell him or herself that they are ok when the reality is, they are broken, crushed, abused. Left to feel dirty, incomplete, and disregarded! No child should ever have to navigate a life in such a way and yet many have and do navigate these roads of life wearing facades of smiles to cover up brokenness. They bear it in silence, in a lifestyle of promiscuity, in consistent unruly behavior patterns, in drug and alcohol abuse all with the hopes of drowning away the fact that their innocence has been marred and no one cared enough to stand up on their behalf.

The beauty in all of this, though not readily seen at the onset, is that God was faithful in keeping and sustaining, growing, and presenting to the world what we have here today – S.H.E. Emerged! My prayer is that this book serves not only as a deep sense of compassion from the eyes and hearts that will read it and take it in, but also a deeper sigh of relief to the souls that have been silently crying and aching to be free from the prisons of trauma they have lived in for years. It is time to heal completely and. It is time to give voice to what has silenced you for so long. It is time to be restored. It is time to be free – free and live in the fullness of the liberty that Christ has granted you! It is time to Emerge!

Chalimar, I pray for you nothing but success on every level of this journey. The fact that you have given voice to things you never thought you could, already makes this a success story. I pray you truly know and understand just how much heaven LOVES you! Stay the course, stay focused and continue pouring out. Be determined to leave here completely emptied of EVERYTHING God sent you here to do! I love you! Xo
Author - TS Brock

Contents

The Beginning of the End

One day she woke up tired, frustrated, defeated, angry, and broken. Tired of fighting. Tired of losing. Tired of working. Angry at what she had allowed to become of her life.

The pain and frustration that she had allowed to consume her heart and flood her mind were the direct result of choices that she had made. You see she had spent a great deal of her life pleasing people, pouring everything she had into being a savior for everyone around her, but neglecting to save herself.

She had fought so hard for the love and admiration of those around her that she forgot to love and admire herself. She did not recognize the beauty, the strength, and the courage it took to even exist. So, in this moment her spirit had reached its breaking point.

This was the beginning of the end. The end of years of neglecting herself abuse both self-inflicted and inflicted by others. It was on this day that her soul had had enough; it was on this day that her heart could no longer carry the weight of the world and the reality that she could no longer champion for anyone else until she championed for herself.

Chapter 1
My Momma, My Daddy and Me

You see, life has not always been kind to her. A young girl was born into humble beginnings. She is a product of teenage parents fighting their way through the world, a world not designed for them to win. A world not kind to them, but nonetheless they fought their way through. So, you see they could only give her what the world had given them which was not much. Love and encouragement were foreign to her opportunities far few and in between. she fought her way through overcoming obstacles clinging to the good and storing the bad. S.H.E was manifesting, S.H.E was emerging from the ashes like a phoenix. S.H.E was me and we had arrived.

My story is not an unfamiliar one. It is the story of a multitude of young black women born in a time and space where the black familial structure was still being redefined. However, it did present with its own unique complexities. My mother was the youngest daughter of six children born into chaos. My grandmother and grandfather had a toxic relationship that ultimately led to him shooting her in the back. She survived but would spend the rest of her life in a wheelchair as a paraplegic, paralyzed from the waist down. My grandmother never complained. She always referred to her injury as God's way to slow her down and bring her to him. She dedicated nearly 50 years of her life to serving

God. She was the epitome of what God desires us to be on so many levels.

I didn't find out how she was injured until I was a teenager. She never taught us anything other than love and respect for my grandfather. He was at almost every holiday gathering and they seemed like two peas in a pod all my life. His wife was always my grandma and my aunts loved my grandmother as if she was their own mother. Talk about walking in love! I wouldn't realize it until I was an adult that she was teaching us the ultimate lesson in walking in love and true forgiveness.

Can you imagine the integrity and strength it took for her to heal and move on from that? That lesson would be one I would need to draw inspiration from in almost every season of my life. I did not know it at the time, but God was using her even in my childhood to teach me what it would take to carry the mantle she would one day leave behind. But her maturity in Christ did not come easy. She faced many trials and tribulations to get to that place. As with any calling God places on your life, there were true tests of the enemy and a multitude of generational curses that would need to be broken. There would be traumas that would follow my mother and her siblings into their adult lives.

As for my mother, her traumas would almost cost me my life. She grew up in what was considered the "country", a rural area just outside of Freehold NJ referred to as Woodsville. Not as developed as the suburb of Freehold that my father had grown up in. My mother was a beautiful woman, striking almost. The ideal woman for that time. She is still revered to this day as one of the "Baddest" women of her time. Coveted for her caramel-colored skin, long jet-black hair, slim physique and beautiful singing voice. I would be a complete contrast to her in every way and was constantly reminded of this. This adoration would contribute to her spiral down a long dark path of failed relationships and drug addiction. So, in a blissful ignorance she embarked on the journey to find a life that she had idealized from things that she had only seen on television or heard stories of while running from her own broken home.

At full speed she hit the ground running. She met a young man that she thought embodied all the things that would bring her a good life. My father was a handsome charismatic young man, with deep dark skin and a 100-watt smile. He was street wise but also business savvy. He had a certain charm about him that made women lose their God given minds. Something I often had a front row seat to see. My father had his own set of traumas to contend with. There was no blueprint for fatherhood for him to follow and his roadmap to manhood was marred with struggle and uncertainty. So unfortunately for my parents, the lack of guidance paired with their immaturity would ultimately decide my fate and at just 18 years old my mother would find herself graduating from high school with me growing in her womb. A few weeks later I would make my entrance into the world on June 28, 1978. And this is where my story begins.

The spite and bitterness my mother had developed for my father motivated her to vainly attempt to hold off labor just to have me on his birthday. Her reasoning was that she fully intended to steal his day from him. However, she ended up giving birth just 2 days before. The epitome of a young black girl lost; my mother did the best she could with what she knew which was not very much. Because of this and because she still had a lot of healing to do, she had not much to give me. Much of my early years are a blur and somewhat unaccounted for.

My mother spent most of her time chasing my dad around town and he spent his time running from her, literally. I have heard countless stories of how she would go upside his head and fight any woman she thought he was involved with. I am sure he allowed her to hit him and out of respect simply restrained her to keep peace. She was feisty and quick with her hands. I often get a good chuckle when I hear stories of her and her "crew" jumping out of cars, chasing my dad up and down the street. Her reputation precedes her. She was hell on wheels so to speak. But the anger and bitterness that she held inside for my father would greatly affect nearly every decision she made for much of her life including how she treated me.

So, it was no surprise that while in pursuit to fill the voids of her life and find the love that she yearned so greatly for that she would find herself pregnant 4 years later with my sister, conceived with my father's best friend at the time and since you cannot build on sinking sand that relationship was over before it even began. This would propel her into what I could only describe as the most toxic relationship she would ever have. A small-town guy with quiet confidence and a dangerous lifestyle. This relationship led to years of drug abuse and ultimately the loss of my mother as I knew her. You see my mother was always chasing a life that she didn't have to work for. She relied on her beauty to get her to where she needed to be. She had and still has today an unrealistic sense of entitlement.

Because of her lack of responsibility, I spent the better part of my childhood moving around from house to house and couch to couch rarely having a stable place to live and living with different family members. This led to my learning how to maneuver life on my own. Unfortunately, my mother was rarely ever held accountable for her behavior. Most family members ignored it or made excuses for it. Granted there were extenuating circumstances that contributed to her behavior that still did not excuse it. Little effort was made to help her heal and deal with her traumas.

As with most African American households' mental illness is discarded or minimized. Black mothers tend to inadvertently destroy their daughters with old wise tales and outdated traditions. They displace their unhealed traumas onto their daughters, ultimately passing them down from generation to generation. Couple that with the lack of knowledge that is shared is a recipe for disaster. These circumstances have created a generation of broken black women and girls.

As a direct result of my grandmothers shooting at the hands of my grandfather a division amongst my mother and her siblings developed. During my grandmother's recovery period they had to be cared for by different family members which gave them a sense of abandonment. As with any family when someone they love is harmed, ill feelings arose toward my grandfather that they did not shield the children from.

Based on studies completed by the National Child Trauma Stress Network. When a child suffers severe trauma, they can have trouble forming attachments. Become unable to regulate their emotions during moments of stress or when triggered and some disassociate themselves from the trauma. Once this skill is mastered, they will "remove" themselves from situations that they deem uncomfortable.

Because my parents had endured so much trauma in their childhoods, they would adopt some of the traits associated with trauma. These traits would influence how they evolved as people and eventually parents. Unchecked trauma will formulate unhealthy habits and inhibited living. Oftentimes people will suppress their trauma and adapt to being functional in their dysfunction. Dysfunctional thought patterns lead to dysfunctional routines and relationships. Your inability to formulate healthy thoughts affects your ability to reason and distinguish between what's good for you and what's not. You don't know what you like, what you love and what truly makes you happy because you're not aware of yourself.

My life was not without some reprieve, now what kind of God would we serve if he did not know and understand that in order to get the best out of us, he must dilute the suffering with moments of joy. My reprieve often came with time spent with my paternal grandmother. She did her best to keep up with me and all of her grandchildren. A lot of what I know about love came from her. She loved me with a love I never had to question. Although Her love did not come without correction, she had such a way with words that even the correction felt like love. She was my mother figure. She was the hope I would cling to over the years. Spending time with her also meant spending time with all of my cousins. Because of her love we grew up more like siblings. Freehold became my village.

Most had no idea what I was really dealing with when I was not there. They only saw the happy child, excited to be with my friends and cousins. They assumed that when I slept over it was because we were friends, not realizing that I probably had nowhere to go that night or when I ate at their homes it was probably because I had not eaten. Freehold will always be my village because being here saved my life on many occasions but God the village kept me.

My father loved me the best way he knew how, but my dad also feared me, feared the parts of me that reminded him of my mother. This would cause our relationship to be strained over the years as it prompted him to discipline me excessively. Now there were moments when discipline was necessary, I was a child with minimal structure going in between various households. That is a recipe for disaster. He did the best he could with what he knew. Overall, we had a great relationship but my father like my mother was dealing with his own traumas from both child and adulthood. My paternal grandmother faced her own set of troubles. She raised 7 children in a racially divided suburb. She was married but not to my grandfather. I can only speculate on how that played out for him as a child. What he knew of how to be a man came from a woman. His upbringing left him with quite a few traumas that would follow him into adulthood.

One trauma that I can speak to happened When I was 8 years old. My father lost his longtime friend to a senseless shooting at the hands of a Freehold Boro police officer. A shooting that would end with the victim running wounded to our home, that day would set into motion the unraveling and ultimately the loss of my father as I knew him. The death took its toll on him and eventually he would succumb to the pressure and mental anguish and check out. He checked out on life and he checked out on me.

Chapter 2
Trauma begets Trauma

Now imagine being a child without a place to call home without the love of your own parents or a sense of belonging. Imagine the very people that were supposed to protect you speaking hateful soul crushing things over your life. Reminding you daily that they were doing you a favor and of how much of an inconvenience it was to have to care for you. Of course, my behavior changed for the worse. I would act out. What child wouldn't? I was scared, alone and felt abandoned. I had to learn quickly how to fend for myself. All things my intermittent caregivers overlooked. It was easier to dismiss me than to have to deal with the truth. That would have required accountability on their behalf for not addressing the traumas that feed my mother's behavior.

Instead of trying to get to the root of my issues they degraded me for them. Painted a false narrative of me simply being disobedient and willful. Never acknowledging the fact that I was homeless, neglected and abused. Unfortunately, that is a common mindset in the black community. They will protect the abuser to save face and hold the victim accountable. There are very rarely any repercussions for the abuser. Only excuses made for their behavior. They are sent away or not permitted to interact with their victims for a period of time. Victims are made to forgive and move on but the wounds are rarely tended and so they remain open.

I would live with my mother in between homes when she was functional. I would often opt to stay with her so that I could look after my sister and truth be told it was easier to deal with her cruelty than everyone else's. For most of my adolescent years I was told I would be just like my mother that I would not amount to anything, that I was no good because I stole to eat and keep clothes on our backs. Go figure a child being persecuted for fighting to live because all the adults around her chose to look the other way rather than challenge my mother. Adults that found it easier to appease her to her face and talk about her behind her back. Adults that placed the ego of a drug addict above the overall needs and safety of children. I would learn later that these adults were operating in guilt. Guilt for the trauma my mother had suffered as a child as well as functioning in their own trauma.

Because of my deep Brown skin like that of my father, I was often referred to as blackie. Family members would make a point of highlighting the fact that I didn't look like my mother and wasn't as pretty as my sister. I had literally become the "black sheep" of my family. These negative connotations would eventually trickle down to their children, who would also take on the attitudes of their parents. This would also make me an outcast amongst my peers.

Adults don't always consider or notice children in the room or within earshot of their conversations. They tend to presume that children lack the comprehension necessary to grasp what is being said. In the black community parents operate under a passed down mantra of "do as I say not as I do" or "what goes on in this house stays in this house" they convince themselves that this means what is being said or done is secure. That is not the case. These conversations led not only to my being outcast due to the sins of my mother but also being demeaned for the color of my skin.

Colorism in the black community has always been an unspoken issue. Although perpetuated long ago on plantations by the separation of the house negro from the field negro based on skin tone. The black community became complacent with the concept until recent years. This is one of those things that would stick with me long beyond its shelf life. It would also define the type of relationship I would have with my maternal family even today.

Now my sister fortunately looked like my mother. Her skin was more of a light honey tone, she had beautiful curly hair and the biggest Brown eyes I had ever seen. In hindsight my hair was equally as long and curly, my eyes were also brown just almond shaped and aside from my skin tone I very much resemble my mother. Because colorism was so ingrained in the very fabric of black people and my maternal family's structure it came easy for them to identify my dark skin as a negative.

In those rare instances that we were together in our mothers care I would find myself caring for both of them. My mother was not a woman who cleaned up after herself. Instead of doing laundry she would just buy new clothes. So, I would find myself cleaning up after all of us. Her boyfriend at the time would cook and clean at times also. He and I had a love hate relationship. I knew and understood who he was and what addiction looked like. That awareness I would later learn was what bothered him about me. He was nice when he was sober but when he wasn't, he was more verbally abusive toward me than anything. In hindsight he was not a bad person. He, like my mother, was just looking for a way out.

Poverty or the threat thereof can strike fear into the heart of even the strongest man. Doing what is right for you but wrong for others under the prying eyes of a child is not something easily done. I believe he loved my mother but like most he found it hard to tell her no. I also believe he knew and understood what it had all cost me. I have always been what I thought was intuitive and there were many moments I can recall him looking at me with such regret and pity. Unfortunately, those moments were fleeting, and human nature prevailed.

One of the few times he did hit me brought about a chain reaction not even I expected. He and my mother were having a disagreement, I was in the room and refused to leave because I believed I needed to protect my mother. Here I stood barley 3ft tall with a fork in hand, with the audacity to challenge him. He slapped me across the face. My mother's only reaction was to send me to my room. I waited for them to go to their room and snuck to the phone. I called my maternal grandmother and told her what had happened. A few hours later my grandmother showed up with my mother's crazy big brother in tow.

He confronted my mother about what I had told my grandmother. She made a feeble attempt to justify the situation and before I knew it, my uncle had slapped my mother so hard she literally slid under my grandmother's car. I stood frozen with my mouth open as my mothers' legs were the only visible part of her body I could see sticking out from under the car. That slap echoed like thunder in my little ears. That day my maternal grandmother packed me up and took me with her for a little while. It was during this visit that she explained to me as best she could to be patient that God had placed a calling on my life, and I may not understand now but one day I would. I looked at her with tears in her eyes, trying to explain to me that my suffering was not in vain. I just hugged her and reassured her that I knew God was going to make it all right.

After that I went to live with my grandmother's best friend who was also her cousin and her children. Her second eldest daughter and I instantly became a duo. She was in high school but I called her mom. Tina showed me a love that will stay with me forever. She loved on me in every way. My hair was always combed, my clothes picked out with care. She encouraged me and made sure I knew I was loved every day but as it was with each good thing in my life at that time it did not last.

My inability to "see" my mother and desire to earn her love and acceptance prevented me from being loyal to anyone but her. I believed that I needed her no matter what the cost. I allowed my mother to manipulate me and being driven by the childish notion that I could save her, I told the school that I got a spanking with a hanger, and they gave me back to my mother. I never forgot Tina or how much she loved me. In hindsight I recognize that I was unable to accept and recognize love in a healthy way because I did not know what that looked like. What Tina tried to give me is what was given to her by her mother. A true mothers love. I regret hurting her in that way. All these years later she and I keep in contact and her daughters call me sister. She will always hold a special place in my heart, and I love her still.

Shortly thereafter my mother moved to Asbury Park. My mother and her companion's addiction became less functional after we moved to Asbury. I was forced to learn new ways to survive. I can remember standing on a chair over a stove frying chicken and making macaroni and cheese out of the box with canned green beans so that we could have dinner. Cooking came easy to me as one of my best skills was being observant. I watched everything, took in my surroundings.

Taking the best parts for myself. I was able to master cooking, cleaning and other domestic skills simply by watching others. As I adjusted to my new surroundings, I would eventually meet two girls whose situation was like mine. Their mother was an acquaintance of my mother, and she would frequently bring them with her to our house. We developed an instant bond forged in the need to survive. We would swap skills; I would help them with their schoolwork and meals at my house after school. They intern taught me how to shoplift. With their help I learned how to push an entire cart of groceries right out the store. I was small for my age.

At 12 I looked to be about 9 years old. Nobody paid attention to a child pushing a shopping cart around a store. They paid even less attention as I pushed it right out the door. I would push the cart home almost 5 blocks and no one questioned me at all. They also taught me how to shoplift clothes and other supplies. My mother never once questioned where any of the stuff came from. After a while she began to look for it. I'm sure she knew what I was doing but she was so consumed with her addiction that I wasn't her priority. Fortunately, God being who he was would send me another reprieve so to speak.

I attended Asbury Park Middle School. There was a secretary that took me under her wing, somehow, she knew that things were not right at home. I would later find out that she too was a God-fearing woman. Another person God had sent to give me some respite. She got together with the principal, Vice Principal, and 2 other teachers. Together they would ensure my sister and I had clean laundry, food and other necessities. God was showing me even then that he had not forgotten about me. I had begun to lose hope and my attempts at suicide had become more frequent.

Although I never discussed them with anyone, I believe they were all aware. I was so small for my age that people often forgot how old I really was. However, one thing would always remind them, I had a huge singing voice. I learned that what I thought I lacked in looks, I had in talent. I could mimic the best of them. At its peak, my voice could reach at least 6-7 octaves high.

Singing and music became my hiding place. I was invited to a small church across the street from the middle school and I immediately joined the choir. Singing became my refuge, my release. When I was singing nothing else mattered and I was unstoppable. My voice was mine, the only thing the world couldn't take away. The teachers made sure to cultivate that gift and encourage me daily. There was one teacher that looked like me, she had long hair with deep dark skin. She looked like a black Barbie doll. She would often remind me that I was beautiful and encourage me to see myself that way. With her encouragement I was about to step outside of my comfort zone.

My 8th grade year I auditioned for the school play, and got the lead as Dorothy in the Wiz, a part I shared with another talented young lady. This would be one of a few positive pivotal moments in my adolescent life. Opening night, I was nervous and disappointed that my mother had not shown up like the rest of the parents to help me prepare. My neighbor was sure to bring my sister. As I peeked out from backstage the principal saw the tears of disappointment streaming down my face. He knew they were due to my mother's absence, and I was getting a sore throat. She had never come to see me sing and this was my moment, a real moment and she had not even bothered to show up. No matter how many times she let me down I could not bring myself to accept it. That toxic desperation would drive me for years.

He gathered some of the other staff and they gave me tea and cough drops to ease the pain in my throat. Once I was feeling up to it the show started, and I mustered up all the confidence and strength I had to go out on that stage. I do not know when she got there but when I started the final scene and began to sing the closing song, Home by Stephanie Mills there she was standing off to the side. Someone from the school had gone and gotten her. Demanded that she come and support me. In that moment that song turned into my plea to be home, not in a structure but home at rest in her love. I sang like my life depended on it and in that moment it did. I needed her to hear me and fully grasp my desperation for her love and acceptance. The next thing I knew everyone was on their feet, clapping and cheering. My mother ran on stage and scooped me up in her arms and for the first time in a long time I felt at home. In my mother's arms. I was home. The moment disappeared as quickly as it came. I did not understand it then but my biggest adversary, my biggest competitor for my mother was one I could never defeat alone. I was battling her addiction and her addiction was winning.

My mother's trauma had created a void in her that I simply could not fill. It was not that she did not love me she did not know how to love me. Her unresolved feelings of abandonment and need to be loved created a contrast of emotions within her. She was constantly at war with herself. I represented love lost and what she could never have from my father. I also represented what she needed, unconditional love. What she felt she never had. My formative years were spent in the midst of her internal war. I would adapt to and absorb these traits. I would become a product of my environment. Her trauma became my trauma. Her traumas destroyed me, and I was left with the task of rebuilding myself.

Chapter 3
Fruit of the Poisonous Tree

The reality of who my mother was and who she was not or would ever be, began to truly take form at one of the lowest moments of my life. It would also be one of the most traumatic. This moment would come when her desire to feed her addiction came at the expense of my dignity and my innocence.

We had a neighbor we thought was just a sweet white lady who is married to a black man. My sister and I would often play with their children at the playground behind our house. She and my mother formed a friendship although she was oblivious to my mother's addiction or so I thought as most people were due to her beauty and charisma. However, her husband, a true predator, was fully aware of her addiction.

So, on this particular day my mother wanted to go out with her friends and get high, so she sent us next door for this woman to watch us as she'd often done. But on this particular day we were all getting ready for bed. She was asleep and her husband came into the room in which my sister, their two sons and myself were getting to bed. He came in calmly, put his hand on my shoulder, looked me square in my eye and said, *it's either going to be you or your sister, you choose. Sleeping here and eating here comes at a price.* At that moment I had to choose whether I should scream, or do I run but I was paralyzed with fear as he had his hand on my shoulder firmly squeezing and I uttered the words *it will be me.*

That night I lost a part of me that I thought I would never get back. He molested me and when he was finished, he smiled at me and told me I made the right choice and told me not to bother to tell anyone because who would believe the child of a crackhead.

I did tell my mother what happened but she dismissed me and told me I had misunderstood. She also reminded me that if I spoke of it again DYFS would come and take me away from her and separate my sister and me. She also said that I would never see her again and she could possibly go to jail.

The fear of being separated from my sister and never seeing her again paralyzed me and I never spoke of it again. Instead, when she went out after that I would opt to stay home alone and watch my sister. I would later find out that his wife was fully aware and that he was abusive to not only her but also their sons. As life would have it, I would see him again many years later as an adult in a grocery store, he stood in front of me frozen and his wife was not far behind. She spoke to me and I could not open my mouth to respond. After a few seconds of staring, he apologized unprovoked, and I simply said I am not your victim! God blessed you and walked away.

In hindsight, that was not a true statement as that particular situation would cripple me as a young woman and a wife.

That summer would be one of the many times I would succumb to the spirit of depression. I would attempt suicide. I took a half-filled bottle of trazodone, my mother's antipsychotic medication.

God was clearly with me. I vomited for hours and slept for a day. Needless to say, I eventually developed bleeding stomach ulcers. Everyone blew it off and attributed it to stress. This summer would also bring about an end to an era in my life. We spent that summer living in her boyfriend's car. Eating canned food and bathing at different store bathrooms. My mother allowed my sister to go stay with her aunt but refused to allow me to go anywhere. By Fall, they had split up and we moved to Freehold to live with my grandmother's sister and her husband.

Being small for my age combined with my dark skin, basically put a target on my back, combine that with my rebellious spirit and poor attitude and well, you could predict what was coming next. I began to fight and act out. I formed unhealthy friendships and relationships that lead to more bad behavior and eventually cost me my freedom.

One fight went too far. As a result, I was sent to a juvenile detention center for months and almost landed in prison, charged as an adult but God once again spared my life. The judge agreed to probation after the charges were reduced and I was released into the care of my uncle as my mother did not even bother to show up for court. I would consequently be expelled from school and barred from the property.

Now my uncle and I had a great relationship and his intentions were good but like my mother he had his own traumas and addictions he was dealing with. I never truly felt welcomed in that household, I was tolerated. My cousin, his daughter and I would fight constantly. I felt bullied and outnumbered but what could I do. I had nowhere else to go. Everything I did was amplified, his wife amplified everything I did and watered down everything my cousin did. It had gotten so bad that my grandmother moved in just to watch over me. I just wanted to fit in somewhere, so I never complained. Eventually I did move in with another cousin and although it started out great it also ended in disaster.

Now I in no way am saying I didn't contribute to some of my own problems, the way that situation ended still lives with me until this day. I am not sure where it took a turn for the worse. A disagreement over a nightgown turned into an all-out war. It was as if they had been waiting for the opportunity to attack me. In the end two people that I thought were supposed to love me, turned on me. I was vilified and lied on so severely that I ended up in a group home. It was unnecessary and just disgusting. That children felt so comfortable destroying another person's life the way they had destroyed mine and not once did the adults even consider that there was something more to the story.

It goes back to what I previously stated. It was the fruit of a poisonous tree. All the negative things the adults had spoken over the years had trickled down to their children. This gave them a sense of superiority over me and allowed them to view me as less than human and beneath them. To them I was disposable. It was like them vilifying me made them less culpable for the things they were doing.

After being released from the group home. My grandmother arranged for me to move to South Carolina with her sister. What I had hoped was going to be a fresh start would turn out to be more disastrous than what I left behind. My aunt lived in a rural area off a long dirt road. Her home was a mid-size modular unit situated on around four or more acres of land. It was beautiful. She was married with two stepchildren. I was excited about the possibility of finally being a part of a family unit. I stepped into this new situation with my best foot forward, but my best just wouldn't be good enough. My aunt worked long hours quite a distance from home. I had registered for school and was working as a waitress at a local diner.

I spent most of my time working and at school. I did my best to keep myself busy and out the way. The less I was seen the less opportunity there would be for trouble. It started off good, but it quickly took a turn for the worse. Because everything was so far away, I would need to learn to drive. My aunt's husband said he would teach me. We would go out and drive up and down the road near the house in the evenings after I got off work.

At first, he was nice making light conversation and him encouraging me that everything was going to work out. By the third week his questions became more personal and almost invasive. This day the energy in the van had changed. I knew this feeling all too well. The next day I declined to go out.

After a week of my declining to go, he went to my aunt and she then demanded that I continue my lessons stating it was too much for them to continue driving me to work and school, she also made clear that I needed to do as I was told. Her tone said what her mouth would not. I felt the sting of being an inconvenience by her words. I reluctantly went back to my lessons. The first few times we went out there was an awkward silence unless I was being instructed.

During the fifth visit it would take a turn for the worse. As we were driving, he started talking, discussing religion and quoting scripture. This was not out of the ordinary because he was a pastor. I just listened and gave minimal answers. He kept going on and on about submission to authority and the will of God. I continued to nod and give one- or two-word answers.

As I approached the area where I would usually make a U-turn, he instructed me to stop the car and put it in park. I assumed he was going to switch seats and take over. He did not get out but kept talking. So, I just listened and occasionally nodded my head. By this time, I had "checked" out of the conversation and my mind was a million miles away. What snapped me back to reality was his hand grabbing my pants. Out of instinct I slapped his hand and asked him was he crazy. He grabbed my wrist and held it tightly. He looked me in the eyes and said, "there are times when you will have to humbly submit to the Will of the Father," I was at a loss for words. While still holding my wrist he said, "this is God's Will" and proceeded to shove his hand down my pants. He then leaned over and tried to kiss me, and I spit in his face. I pushed him away and got out of the van. I walked home. I went straight to my room and locked the door.

He did not attempt to speak to me for some time after that. I attempted to tell my aunt, but she dismissed me and told me I was just a troubled child. She did however allow me to go to her mother in law's house when I was not at work until she came home in the evenings for a few weeks. I was at a loss. There was nowhere for me to go back home in New Jersey. I was trapped and abandoned by my family. What was I going to do? I shut my mouth and stayed.

The abuse got worse, and she began to treat me terribly. I eventually just left. I stayed with some members of the church for a few days and then moved in with a friend from school. With no driver's license it was hard to get around, which made it difficult to keep my job or get to school. I would eventually buy a train ticket and go back to New Jersey. I would rather take my chances in a familiar setting and that's what I did.

I would not speak to my aunt again for over 20 years. I did tell my grandmother what happened. She did not give me much, just her same positive spin. I took it because at least she didn't call me a liar.

Needless to say, from that point on I lost faith and trust in people for a long time.

Although I have forgiven them and moved on, those memories will always bring with them a little tinge of hurt. They preyed upon my situation and the vulnerable position I was in. I was easy prey. There was no one to hold them accountable. I was a child without a home or parents. I was damaged and came from a troubled background. They were upstanding God-fearing people. Who was the world going to believe?

Chapter 4
Spiraling

As life moved on so did I or so I thought. My teenage years would prove to be as tumultuous as my adolescence. I spent most of it trying to find my place and my way while still living from house to house and couch to couch. In between just trying to maneuver my own growth and development. Still trying to take care of my mother and my sister the best way I could and take care of myself the only way I knew how. My sister did eventually go and live with her father, but I always felt in some way responsible for her. When I look back over my life there are so many moments that I can recall where my desire to belong and to be the savior, the hero for my mother and my sister that were just so toxic. And this is where those traits truly settled in and took root. Traits that I would carry into my adulthood. It was these habits and desires that would dictate years of self-inflicted stress strain and pain. There were moments where I had choices.

My grandmothers would often step in, and I would live with them intermittently, but my mother would never let me stay gone for long. She had come to depend on me being responsible as much as I had come to depend on her needing me in some capacity good or bad. So, I would find myself walking back into the toxic storm that was her life because I so desperately needed her love and approval. I was determined to save her from herself from her surroundings from her addiction. Not realizing that this drive to save her would cost me something. I was a child searching for the love that she could never give me because it was never given to her in the way she needed. She did not love me; she did not know how. I was simply one of the few things she had control over. This trait or behavior would show up in how I managed relationships. I treated people like they were expendable and if I could not control the narrative, I had no use for them.

My paternal grandmother had always been my rock. I thought she would live forever. She was always there trying to hold all the pieces together. I never knew that for a good portion of my life she was fighting for her own life. When I was taken to the hospital to visit her, I never imagined it would be my final moments with her. I was 17 and ignorant to things like cancer. She was strong and she would win this battle as she had won so many others. Right? She had to, but she would not. Although cancer wouldn't win, a side effect would, and I would lose her on a cold December day. As if I hadn't suffered enough. I now had to learn to live without the one person who had never failed me.

I would grieve the loss of her for many years to come. My trauma level was nearing doomsday levels and no one even noticed. Up until this point addiction was not an issue for me as I knew and understood how it had affected my life. However, while going through my grandmother's room, I found a pack of cigarettes hidden under her air conditioner. That day I smoked every one of them. I had never smoked anything before in my life but that day I just wanted something of hers to hold onto, even if it was more toxic. The impact of losing her stayed with me throughout my adult life. I grieved for her almost daily.

It wouldn't be until my late 30's that I would fully come to terms with her death.

Chapter 5
Blind Ambition

I became a mother at the age of 19 and would go on to have my second child by the age of 21. While staying with some family in Trenton NJ I met my eldest daughter's father. What we thought was love was merely friendship and codependency because we understood each other. He was the best person he could be for me which wasn't much because we were still just 2 lost young people trying to carve out our place in the world. It was all fun and games until I found out I was pregnant. He never mistreated me. I was probably harder on him than he was on me. My inability to form emotional attachments prevented me from seeing him as anything more than a distraction from the life I was running from. By the time I met him I was literally hell on wheels. It was me against the world. I was going to do it my way no matter who got hurt because nobody cared about my feelings.

And the baby makes 3! I went through a multitude of emotions from fear to doubt to panic. There was one thing I was certain about and that was that I would have my baby. We bounced around, stayed with different family members, struggling to find a place of our own but we were two kids about to have a kid. What was I going to do with a baby? I could not bring a baby into this street life. Something in me knew that something was going to have to change for the safety and sake of this child that was coming one way or the other. I knew he was not ready to be a father. Me being selfless and ever the protector of everyone but myself made the decision that it would be best for both of us if I just disappeared and that is what I did. I called the one person I knew would show up for better or worse. I called my mother. She was there to pick me up an hour later. I just left. I didn't even take my things. I moved back to freehold pregnant alone and scared but the survivor in me would not let me give up. I decided that my child would never suffer like I suffered. That my child would have the mother that I never did and have a life that I was never afforded. That was the plan in my head. Executing that plan would prove to be an entirely different journey.

Truth is I didn't have the necessary tools to be a better parent because my trauma and inherited traumas were still governing my life. I never contacted him again and it would be well after the birth of our daughter that his uncle would track me down and show up at my aunt's house to see his great niece. I would eventually take her to see her father and his family was always welcoming and did all they could for her. In hindsight I should have given him more credit because he absolutely loves his daughter.

My pregnancy was difficult. I was high risk and had developed preeclampsia. I was being seen weekly by my OBGYN and monthly by my specialist. Around the sixth month of my pregnancy, I went to my monthly doctor's appointment with my specialist for my vaginal ultrasound. It seems this child I was carrying was camera shy and would only allow pictures of her backside. After finally seeing the front of this child and hearing her heartbeat, I was told that there was a possibility that my child would have Down syndrome. I was devastated to say the least. The first thought in my mind was how could God just keep allowing me to suffer. The specialist immediately encouraged me to terminate as they felt that I would be unable to care for a child with special needs. I called my aunt hysterically crying and boy did she read them the riot act. I refused, and I was determined to have the love that I deserved and have somebody to love. So, I moved in with an aunt who had a son with Down syndrome so that I could learn how to care for my baby.

She wasted no time preparing me. She gave me full charge of my little cousin and boy was he busy. Derrick was energetic and full of life. He had such a gentle spirit and playful nature about him. Spending time with him and caring for him erased any doubt I had in my mind that I was up for the challenge. Other than some physical limitations Derrick was highly functional. He attended school and was intelligent. He was also very mischievous. I can remember one time he opened the front door and hid in the bushes while I was in the bathroom. I panicked, running through the house calling his name, with his little brother my Godson in toe. When I finally noticed the front door open, I went out and began to call his name. As I am walking back and forth up the street, I hear giggling coming from the bushes. I looked down and there he was laughing a long hearty laugh at my expense.

Between caring for him and my Godson I was getting all the practice I needed. This would prove to be another pivotal moment as it was at this point that I was able to see what a mother truly does and what a mother's love truly feels like. I got to see what it looks like. I spent my days chasing behind two busy little boys and in my free time nesting, talking to my baby making plans and sharing my hopes and dreams for her future with her. But like most things in my life that time would come to an end. I would go into labor on a cold February morning while at a doctor's appointment. I thought I had gas. I asked the nurse for some tums; she went to get them but something stopped her. She turned around and placed a hand on my belly, smiled and said you do not have gas you are in labor. She told me to have a seat but instead I wandered off to find a sandwich, I was hungry. Ten minutes later I would hear my name being called over the intercom of Monmouth Medical Center in Long Branch ordering me to report to labor and delivery.

The nurse must have called my aunt, who in turn called my mother. By the time I made it to the L&D floor my aunt was waiting for me and none too pleased with my antics. After changing my clothes and putting on a gown, I walked the halls to get this baby moving as I had refused the epidural. My fear of that needle outweighed the pain of the contractions I was having. My mother and stepfather showed up just in time. As they were setting me up on the table to check my cervix, she came strutting in wearing a black sheer blouse, leather mini skirt and 6-inch black leather pumps.

I asked her where she was coming from, she said "home I had to dress for the occasion". She walked over to the bed with such authority that it was comedic when she looked down and saw the crown of Asante's head making its way out. The next thing I know is she's passed out on the floor. Where she stayed until I was finished. So, with my Aunt Cheryl holding my legs, my mother passed out on the floor. My Asante made her grand entrance into the world that evening. My baby girl had arrived perfect in every way 7lbs 6oz 21.5 inches long and to God be the glory she did not have Down syndrome. She would develop sleep apnea and had to wear a monitor for the first year of her life. By year 2 she had outgrown the condition and was off the monitor. God had created a situation to allow me to learn the skills I would need to care for this new life properly.

She's here and now I have this baby. What do I do? Now the real work begins. Where do I begin, I spent the first few months of her life living in a rooming house with my mother and because of our toxic relationship the good times never lasted for long. You see my mother had convinced herself that she was somehow entitled to raise my child so that she could redeem herself for all that she had not done for my sister and me. Never in my wildest dreams did I see what transpired next coming.

My sister and I are four years apart and while I were an adult and out of the system there was still an open case with the division of youth and Family Services for her. So, on what was supposed to be the last day of my sister's case and the final visit I happened to be present with my baby. I excused myself and went to visit one of my mother's "neighbors" to get out of the way. I also had developed a strong disdain for this woman over the years as she dropped the ball on our case and rarely ever did her job effectively. She didn't even realize she had been bamboozled by a child. Whenever she was scheduled to visit, I always ensured that the house was cleaned, my mother was sober and there was food on the stove. She asked the bare minimum questions and often just took my mother's word for everything.

After concluding my sister's visit, my sister came to find me, so I assumed she was gone. Upon entering the room, she approached me and asked how I was doing, she then looked at my baby, smiled and left. Seven days later I would receive a notice from the courts and the division of youth and Family Services informing me that an emergency hearing had been held and it had been decided that because I was never taught the basic parenting skills needed to raise a child with health issues that it was in my daughters' best interest to be removed from my care. Unbeknownst to me my mother had set these events in motion. She foolishly thought that because she was my mother that they would give my daughter to her. She danced with the devil and he stepped not only on her toes but mine.

They removed my child from my care for eight exceptionally long weeks. At one point even placing her up for adoption. But you see God was always in the midst. I hired an attorney with the help of my stepfather and worked two jobs to cover the cost. I moved in with my grandmother's sister in-law as she had an 11-bedroom home that would afford me the space I needed to get my daughter back. Aunt Cynthia was such a sweet and gracious woman. She helped and supported me throughout the entire process.

My room had an additional smaller room attached so that Tweet as we affectionately called her would have her own space. I made it a point to attend to every detail of her room with care. Everything was decorated with Elmo. Her closet was full of clothes in every size as well as cases of milk and baby food. Her Godparents made sure that whatever she needed was available to her. The love and support they showed was and still is priceless. Donna and Ty never turned their backs on me. They have stood by me for over 23 years. I could not have asked for better

Godparents for my daughter. I would leave nothing to chance. I missed my baby so much it hurt.

One day while working at my day job which was Toys R Us. The foster mother who had my child came in to do some Christmas shopping and as God would have it, she pushed her cart right up to my register and there was my baby staring back at me squirming and squiggling to get out of the cart and get to me. The woman looked at me and said with certainty you must be her mother. As the tears filled my eyes I nodded yes, and she took my baby out of the cart and handed her to me. She stayed in the store for over an hour allowing me to spend time with my child. When it was time for her to go, she assured me that she would be going to court and speaking on my behalf as my child had stopped eating and completely withdrew and she was sure it was due to her being separated from me. She said, "based on today I can say with certainty that this child is loved and should have never been taken from you". By the next court hearing the following month they had removed my child from that foster mother and placed her in another home out of town under the guise of adoption.

However, as God will do what only he can, the judge took issue with this and ordered them to allow me full contact visits immediately. For the next month I would go to the office and sit with my daughter. I would bring her clothes and toys and play with her for hours. By the final court date or what was supposed to be the final court date this worker was still trying to find reason to not return my daughter as she felt she had failed my sister and I and she was not going to fail my daughter. But you see someone was praying for me, my grandmothers who had always covered me in prayer. And although my paternal grandmother had transitioned on, I knew that her prayers were still covering me.

At the next court date, my lawyer Bettina Munson argued that the merits of their case were based solely on my mother's words and that the worker had and is abusing her power. The judge agreed and ordered them to return my child that day or be charged with kidnapping. He would also make clear that the case had no merit and was to be closed immediately. They argued that due to the length of separation that they be allowed at least a 30-day window to monitor the transition. The judge agreed but I had other plans. They would never get that close to my child ever again if I had my way. After 8 long weeks I was reunited with my baby girl.

As life would have it during all of that I had met someone and was having baby number 2. Because of all that I had gone through over the past few months there was still a level of fear that resided in me and make no mistake the worker did not take the loss graciously. She continued to harass me, she would call Asante's pediatrician and all her specialists. I switched to a new children's hospital, and she accused me of medical neglect assuming I missed the appointment. When that did not work, she filed for another extension of the 30-day monitoring. My lawyer made sure that this wouldn't hinder my relocating.

The judge made clear that if I left the state of NJ that my case would be closed. With that promise in my mind, I made the decision I felt would best protect my children. I packed my bags and moved to Perry Florida. It was during this chapter of my life that God allowed me to see what was possible. The people, places and things that I would encounter on this new journey are responsible for changing the way I saw living. You see the light at the end of the tunnel was not just being able to provide for my children it was making a home wherever we were.

I got a small 2-bedroom apartment modestly decorated. Although it wasn't a mansion it was ours. I was surrounded by women whose small apartments looked like something straight out of a magazine. These women were not afraid of working at the local fast-food restaurant if they were able to provide for their children. This was foreign to me. Because where I was from it was taboo to work at such places, where I was from it was considered shameful to lower yourself to work at a fast-food restaurant. But these women took pride in being able to go to work, provide a decent and comfortable home for their children and put food on the table doing just that. In the short time that I resided in Florida I would learn so much not just about life but about myself. I learned that I was capable, I learned that I was strong, I learned that I was beautiful, and I learned that I was worthy. I found work and in time fully furnished my 2-bedroom apartment. I had learned how to manage my money and provide a comfortable home and life for my children.

When I finally went into labor with my second child, she came into this world eyes wide open and full of vigor. My Shakayla was born partially in an elevator at Tallahassee Memorial Hospital, in Tallahassee Fl. 6lbs 7oz 19.5 inches long. She wasted no time making her presence known, making her needs known ever demanding all traits that would follow her throughout her young life. It was interesting how the roles would be reversed as she progressed. She was a complete contrast to her big sister who was more laid back and quiet. In time she became the big sister. She began to walk at nine months and from that moment to now she has been dragging her big sister around by the hand leading her through life with love, caring and kindness. It is with that same care and loving kindness that she would lead her mother one day.

Unfortunately, my life in Florida would be cut short by my toxic attachment to my mother. My mother had a penchant for interrupting my life whenever it was going well as if she were afraid that I would accomplish something that she was never able to. It seemed that she feared me growing up and becoming my own woman because that would mean that I would be unavailable to her. This had become a pattern with her from childhood. Whenever I would be in a comfortable home with someone who genuinely cared for me, she would always show up and take me back. Something she rarely did to my sister. I remember living with my cousin for a brief stint. Her mother was a nurse and although a little obnoxious her intentions were good.

While living with her she put me in dance, I did gymnastics and participated in all shore chorus. This woman put a lot of effort into showing me something different. An opportunity arose for my cousin and I to apply to Petty Preparatory school. She took the application to my mother and asked her to sign it. After hearing what it would entail my mother said no. She stated that she would not allow me to go live on a school campus. Well needless to say that turned into a full-blown argument that ended with my mother slapping her and that ended my residency in that household.

So, this situation being no different after visiting me and seeing how well I was doing I received a phone call from her two months later informing me that she had been diagnosed with a brain aneurysm. She had not only informed me of this but she had informed my sister. My sister called me voice full of fear, hysterical crying begging me to come back to make sure that our mother would be OK and receive the care that she needed. Once again that toxic attachment would disrupt my life. I packed my bags, broke my lease, loaded my two babies into a car and drove the 32 hours back to New Jersey. This time would be different because I not only had one child, but I also had two.

I stayed with a cousin for a few weeks and then I realized that that was not going to work, and I needed space of my own. I made the decision to enter a transitional housing program called the linkages. While in the program I met a woman, who was the director of the program. She recognized the highly toxic nature of my relationship with my mother.

After we learned that my mother had exaggerated her condition, her awareness was heightened. So, she took special care to sow into me she tried her best to help me heal. She gave me a piece of advice that I still carry with me today. She said, "you have to do what you have to do for self-preservation". And until you get to that place your mother will always have the power to disrupt your life. While in the program I took the teachings and training very seriously because I was always self-aware, and I knew that there were things that I needed and skills that I lacked. My desire to be the best mother that I could be propelled me headfirst into learning those skills.

I immediately enrolled in classes to get my GED and picked up a part time job through Job Corps. After completing the courses for my GED through Job Corps I was able to enroll in classes for my CNA license. I would catch the bus on route 33, get off on route 66, walk my children to the babysitter, walk back down the Hill, get on the bus and catch it into Asbury Park to go to work and then to Ocean Township to class. By 4:30 I will be running to catch the last bus to get my children from the sitter on one side of the highway, then catch the bus to the program on the opposite side. It was the longest nine months of my life.

One of the biggest moments of that time was being invited to walk with the graduating class of 2001 to receive my high school diploma with my two babies by my side. Unfortunately, my mother could not even allow me to have this moment. It was one of the rare instances that I was able to have both of my parents in the same space for something positive. However, the toxicity that resided in her could not let the day go by without her having a moment.

While I was on the field preparing to walk across the stage, she sat in the stands and consumed an entire bottle of gin. When the ceremony was over, she noticed my father was there and proceeded to make a scene. I tried to redirect her by asking for a few pictures but to no avail she began to berate him and accuse him of being abandoning me. Yes, right there on the field, screaming at the top of her lungs in front of everyone. My father not wanting to be the cause of ruining my moment turned and walked away. I spent the rest of the day sulking and disappointed. She did not even go to dinner with us. Despite her continued antics I successfully completed the program and completed my CNA training. I also walked away with rental assistance.

While searching for a place I moved in with my mother temporarily and found a job as a CNA and a second job at a Burger King near the house. I had also registered for the nursing program at Brookdale Community College. It took me almost five months to find an apartment that met the specifications outlined by the state. During this time, I would be exposed to more and more of my mother's behavior. In preparation for my move, I never cashed my checks from Burger King, and I had also received a sizable refund from a financial aide at school. I would hide my checks in the mattress of the futon I slept on.

One day while going to tally up what I had earned so to ensure I could cover my security deposit and get furniture I noticed that some checks were missing. I immediately turned the space upside down looking for my missing checks. While doing so my mother walked in the door and I asked her if she had seen my checks. she stared at me defiantly looking me straight in the eyes and said, "So what I took them you have more than enough, those few little checks won't make or break you".

The rage and anger that arose in my chest scared me because not only had she taken that money from me she had taken that money from my children. Before I knew it, I had lunged at her but before I could get to her, her baby brother came through the door. He immediately put me in a bear hug, and she ran out the door. After I explained what she had done, he took her to task, even snatching her in the collar. He did get her to tell him where she took my checks to. All but 1 that is. As I took inventory of my uncashed checks, I also noticed that she had taken my tuition reimbursement check. I immediately walked down to the check cashing place knowing fully that is where she went to cash them and reprimanded them as well as demanding that they refund my money as her name was not on the checks and they had no right to do that, I also informed them that I would be calling the police. It took a few weeks, but the owner did eventually refund my checks but could not account for my tuition reimbursement check. It was at this point that I would meet my first husband.

I was sitting on my mother's porch trying to figure out how I would come up with the money for my security deposit. When this guy walks up, brown skin, bald head around 6ft tall with an amazing smile. He asked me my name. I asked him why and he asked me if I was Lynn's daughter and I replied yes. He said I think I may have something that belongs to you. He handed me an envelope and inside the envelope was my tuition reimbursement check. She had signed the check and given it to him as collateral to buy drugs. He stated that he did not feel good about it and had been looking for me for weeks to return it.

After that day he and I would become friends. We would sit and talk on the porch for hours. We would hang out, go out to eat, often walking by the beach and just sharing our hopes and dreams with one another. We discovered we shared a love for music. He was an aspiring Hip Hop artist and was a part of a group that ran a recording studio. I would accompany him to the studio and sometimes sing or write a hook for their tracks. Our love for music only deepened our connection. However, it would also prove to be one of the things that would come between us.

During this time, I would purchase my first car. A white station wagon with no radio. The Batmobile as it was affectionately called by family and friends. It was an accomplishment nonetheless and one that I was proud of. But like anything that was a source of pride for me it created a source of resentment for my mother. Two months after I purchased the car, she would throw a temper tantrum because I would not give her money and she smashed out the front and passenger side windows of my car. I called my father who immediately sent over a traveling glass company to fix the windows. Upon his arrival to have the windows fixed she attempted in a fit of rage to assault him with a box cutter but only ended up hitting Shakayla in the face leaving a permanent scar under her eye. At this point I went to social services and explained that I could no longer stay there while waiting to find housing and they placed my children and I in a hotel. It was a temporary stay as a few weeks later we would move into our new home in Asbury Park, New Jersey.

It was a mid-size 2 family house with two bedrooms and an eat-in kitchen, living room, 1 bathroom and a large backyard. I was so excited to be moving into our new home. I paid all my bills in advance with the money I had saved and took extensive care to decorate and furnish our new home. I remember searching several different stores to find glow in the dark paint so that I could paint the girl's room and put the constellations on the ceiling. I bought an iron and wood bunk bed set, put power puff girl decals all over the walls with the coordinating bedding and filled their room with toys. For myself I chose an iron 4 post canopy bed and covered it with red and black bedding and an overabundance of throw pillows.

For my kitchen I found a white and black lacquer dining table with the matching bar trimmed in leather with a piano made of mirrors on the front. In my living room I chose light gray microfiber furniture, painted the walls a beautiful shade of rose pink and accented them with a gray border and grey Vertical Blinds. I took such care to decorate our home so that it would be comfortable. Because my upstairs neighbor was elderly and never used the backyard, she allowed me exclusive use of it. I went out and purchased a swing set and swimming pool for the backyard along with a grill and patio table. This would be our home and I would do everything I could to ensure that my children had the life that I was never afforded.

Kenny and I would continue to speak here and there but I was focused on working and providing for my children which left little time for anything else. On the off chance that I had time, we would meet up at the recording studio and spend time together there. I submerge myself into my children in every way, ensuring they would have all that they needed. My schedule changed to overnights so that I could be a full-time mother during the day, and I would work double shifts on the weekends to ensure that financially they would never want for anything. I tried my best to find the strength to create distance between my mother and I as God had begun allowing me to see her for who and what she was.

I saw more of her, I tried to change more of me, a change was stirring on the inside. As I became more and more invested in these lives that I had been blessed with I found less and less value in holding on to her. I now had 2 little people who loved me unconditionally and I loved them just as much if not more. This infuriated her and she would occasionally lash out and throw temper tantrums or try to create some unnecessary chaos in my life, but I managed to stand firm in my position and distance myself from her as best I could. Little did I know or even understand physical distance was not the answer as I had embodied the very traits, I was trying to get away from, but this next chapter would bring about something and someone I had never known existed. God was going to make his presence known.

Because Kenny and I had grown somewhat apart due to my work schedule. I began dating someone else. Although I continued to record with him a relationship was not the focus. He had become more interested in my talent and trying to find ways to utilize it to propel his own career. This allowed space for my new relationship to grow. To respect his privacy, I will call him J. J and I had a lot of fun together. Like most of my relationships, I served a purpose. I immediately slipped into the role of nurturer. I helped him get focused and find a job. Supported his growth and did my best to be whatever he needed but because of my inability to form emotional attachments he felt my mind and heart were elsewhere. He hated the time I spent at the recording studio and was jealous of my relationship with the team. Because of the emotional distance and plain immaturity, he began sleeping with someone else. Well, we all know the world is small.

The woman he cheated with was a coworker who happened to be from my hometown of Freehold NJ. It didn't take long before the news was brought to my attention. When I confronted him about it of course he lied but I found receipts with her name on them for things she had paid for. I eventually stopped asking and he assumed I believed him. He never realized my silence was deadly and that it did not mean I was over it. It meant that I was being vengeful. Because I knew that my time at the studio bothered him, I began to go more. I would stay later than normal and began coming home at odd hours. This drove him nuts.

We would have frequent disagreements about it, but I was on a mission. I then found out about another woman he was cheating with. He had gotten bold. She lived right across the street. At this point I put him on notice that 2 could play that game but he would learn I was better at. I started going out on dates and made it known that is what I was doing. His ego was at its wits end with me, but he stayed around. He stopped going to work and would sit outside the studio waiting for me to come out. We would look down from the window and watch him sit there. The team would ask me why I was being so mean, and I would laugh and say that is what he deserved for cheating. Kenny would fuss at me and tell me my behavior was immature and to stop it. The final straw was finding out the woman across the street was pregnant. Now I was going to break him as he was clearly trying to do to me. Those unhealthy traits were in full gear. I am not excusing his behavior; I am just saying the right thing to do would have been to simply breakup and move on but in my mind he did not deserve easy. On the last night of our relationship, he came over as I was getting dressed to go out. I knew he would show up and was purposely getting dressed up in front of him. He asked where I was going, and I simply replied out. He attempted to assert some authority by telling me I was not going anywhere. I laughed. Who was he to tell me anything? I continued to get dressed and waited for my sitter to arrive. He sat in the living room as if he were really going to stop me.

My date arrived and text my phone to let me know he was outside. I grabbed my purse and walked out the door. J came out behind me and tried to stop me. I pushed him aside, looked him in the eyes and told him I owe him nothing. I also let him know I knew about the baby. There he stood mouth wide open. I called him a dummy and got in the car with my date, and he pulled off. Now what he did not know was that I was not actually going on a date. The guy that picked me up was a friend of one of my aunts and I was going to a party at their house but in my mind, he deserved to suffer, and I was going to see to it that he did. When I returned home, he was still there asleep. I got ready for bed and slept on the couch.

The next morning, I put on MJB's My Life album and started my Saturday morning cleaning. When he finally got up, he realized that I was not just cleaning, I was sweeping him and his stuff right out of my house. I was done playing this came and the night before was my final move on the chessboard. My goal was to ensure he left exactly how he had arrived in my life. With nothing. He had lost his job and his car by this point. Now she can have you. Checkmate!

Chapter 6
A Wedding

Two years into living in our new home Kenny and I would decide to take our relationship to the next level, and we begin seriously dating. I couldn't see it then, but I was operating just as my mother had. Especially when it came to relationships. I was so focused on creating this ideal "family" that I skipped right over the healing. Had I known then what I know now I would have never dated Kenny. He was a great friend but neither of us was prepared to live as husband and wife. We did not even understand what that level of commitment truly meant. We would date seriously for another year before we decided to move in with one another.

I was earning more money and finally saved up enough to purchase another car. This was also around the time that he convinced me that we should move to Ocean County where we would have more house for less money. I did not see the red flag in this because I was so blinded by my drive to create this life for my children that I did not have that I never really asked myself what his motives truly were. Although my gut said no, I packed up my children and we found a beautiful ranch style home in Lakewood NJ. Little did I know happily ever after was not just around the corner. You see hurt people hurt people and the truth of the matter was that I just created another codependent situation. I thought that I could save him. I thought that I could heal him but oh was I wrong.

Our relationship would be a tumultuous one. His family was amazing, very loving and giving people but not without their own issues as with any family. I got along well with his mother and siblings and became awfully close to one of his cousins. Shalonda, Shan would grow to be one of my best friends and losing her to kidney disease a few years later was devastating. After about seven months of living in our new home Kenny proposed and I happily said yes for all the wrong reasons. You see we were both running from the people we were always told we would be, running from all the negative connotations that were associated with our very being from people who chose not to speak life into us but to speak hell and damnation over us.

Both of us came from single mothers who had become so dependent on our care of them that they would rather see us suffer then to see us happy because if we were suffering, we would be accessible to them. Our marriage was never built on the right things. We thought that we could make right all the wrongs we had suffered as children and over the course of our lives by creating something we could call our own. Something that just wasn't meant to be. Had we looked at and paid attention to who we really were we would have known that we could be no good to one another because we were no good for ourselves. For how he could be a husband when he had yet to learn how to be a man, he was not raised to be anything other than a support for his mother and her crutch and I was not taught to be a wife and everything I knew about being a woman I taught myself. How could I give something when I had no idea what it was, I was supposed to be giving? I didn't know what love was. I did not even know how to love myself. I was simply going through the motions mimicking what I saw.

One of the most frustrating aspects of our marriage would be our sexual incompatibility. He lacked the basic emotional understanding to deal with a woman who had suffered sexual trauma and he desired an aspect of me that I simply could not give him. I didn't know it then, but we lacked intimacy. He did not know my love language because I did not know it and I most certainly did not know his. There was still a great deal of healing that needed to come but I did not know how to heal. We just simply could not give each other what we did not have to give but we pressed on anyway because we had a point to prove. We were going to prove to the world that we were worthy of love and capable of living "normally" or what society considered normal. This lack was the direct effect of my never being taught how my body functions. Not understanding my sexuality or even feeling in control of it.

At the same time my father had begun to change his own life and had come full circle. He had overcome his issues and was on the path to healing. He had even gotten married. A part of his rebuilding of himself was taking classes and investing in real estate. So as part of our reconnection he offered us a home in Neptune NJ. A beautiful bi-level four bedroom 2 1/2-bathroom home. He even custom painted every room to my specifications. We were spending time together, we were getting reacquainted, and I had finally gotten to a place where I was able to forgive him because I now understood him. So, with the pending engagement we moved to Neptune into a better home and planned our wedding. Never once Did I pay attention to the signs, never once Did, I pay attention to what God was trying to tell me because I was so consumed with this ideal that I had in my mind.

So full steam ahead I planned and executed this beautiful $11,000 wedding complete with a $3000 wedding gown and a wedding party of 16. Again, everything that could go wrong went wrong. The septic system backed up on the lawn. It rained at 6:00 o'clock that morning so my outdoor ceremony had to be moved indoors. I forgot to get my hair and nails done and one of my maids of honor had to be sewn into her dress. But nonetheless we pressed forward because like most people when things go wrong, I assumed it was the enemy just trying to block my blessing. But the truth of the matter is it was God because he knew that we were unequally yoked he knew that this was not what he had for me, and he wanted me to know that he had not sanctioned this union.

My future husband and I had completely different religious views and backgrounds one thing that has always been a constant in my life is the church. No matter where I was in my life there was always a church I knew the Bible I knew the word from a very young age my maternal grandmother had also prophesied over my life many times that there was this calling on me but when you're caught up in the moment of life we often tend to get in our own way and this was one of those moments where I got in my own way and moved out of God's timing. So, we moved forward, and we had this wedding and what should have been a beautiful day was a disaster from start to finish. He was offended when my father's family waited outside for Aunt to arrive. He felt she didn't acknowledge him. He again did not understand that my father's family is a matriarchy not a patriarchy. She picked up my paternal grandmother's mantle. We give her the respect she has earned.

My maternal grandmother pulled me to the side at the wedding and told me you know this is not your husband. Although I pretended to ignore her, smiled, kissed her on the cheek and told her I loved her. I walked away knowing deep down inside that she was right. My father also knew but as our relationship was still new and fragile, he walked me down the aisle anyway, with tears streaming down his face to Donny Hathaway for All We Know. Whispering in my ear to slow down reminding me that there is no rush. I have never clung to my daddy as tightly as I clung to him that day as I felt the deeper meaning of his words, but pride and my own stubborn nature would not allow me to look back.

As the evening progressed, of course my mother could not just be happy. As per usual she created a scene, but this time she had a partner. His mother, whom we affectionately called nanny. The two of them decided that they would not support our marriage and left in a cab after they made their little announcement.

I watched as our guests celebrated us and it was as if I was having an out of body experience and everyone was moving around me, moving past me and I was in a state of suspension. I felt something coming. It would not be until many years later that I realized that this feeling that made my stomach flip upside down this sense of knowing the visions all meant that I operated in the gift of the prophetic. Something was coming but my mind was clouded, and I was unable to see what God was trying to show me. One of the guests that had attended our wedding was an ex-girlfriend of Kenny's who was also my hairdresser, a few guests came in to tell me she was outside upset. While we were inside celebrating, she was outside consumed with what I could only assume was regret and shock that he had moved forward with the wedding. We continue to celebrate and at the end of the night we packed up the decor and went back to our house. I was his wife, he had chosen me, right?

Chapter 7
God's Hail Mary

Around 2:00 AM his phone started to ring, and he looked and ignored it. It rang at least 15 times and he refused to answer it. I would eventually roll over and tell him to answer the phone and as I spoke those words there was a loud knock at our front door. I got up to answer it and he grabbed me and told me not to. I pushed him away and said I'm going to answer. I put on my robe and slippers and went to the front door and lo and behold there was his ex-girlfriend standing on our doorstep tears streaming down her face and he was standing at the top of the stairs as I held the door open and looked in between both. He told her to leave, and I invited her in.

My thought process was if she came here to get something that belongs to her then by all means take what is yours. She came into the house, and I went and sat in the kitchen. He immediately grabbed her by the arm and escorted her back out the front door. I picked up the phone and called my cousin and maid of honor Shakita in shock and went downstairs to the half bath. I climbed up on the toilet and cracked the window so that we could hear as the two of them argued back and forth about how our wedding had even happened. But foolish pride will make you overlook even the most obvious of situations.

Our marriage was over before it had even begun but my foolish pride allowed me to continue to press forward in a situation that God had not ordained for me. After about 15 minutes of arguing she left. I came upstairs and went into our bedroom and got back into bed. He walked in behind me and attempted to explain but I shut him down and told him "If that is where you want to be then by all means go. But if you choose to stay, I never want to speak about it again". When I think back to that moment, I could kick my own behind. Like sis what were you thinking! The answer is I wasn't. God had thrown me a Hail Mary and I botched the play.

I was on a mission to control the narrative of my children's lives. I would give them everything I felt they deserved at all costs, even if the cost were me. Needless to say, he stayed and over the course of our 10-year journey there were many highs and lows. It was a bumpy ride for sure. Now that's not to say that we did not have some form of love for one another because we genuinely loved each other as people but when you don't know how to love yourself you can't possibly love someone else and when you are bleeding and wounded, if left open to fester make no mistake that you will bleed on everyone around you and bleed, we did!

We spent 10 years bleeding on one another trying to force a relationship and build a marriage on a faulty foundation that was not sanctioned by God. Both of us tried to be compatible with one another when we were not. Me foolishly trying to love him out of his dark places and him trying to love me into submission. You cannot submit to something that you do not fully trust, and I didn't trust him.

I didn't trust his love for me. I did not believe him but out of blind ignorance I stayed. Fear of failure, the shame of having to say that I could not make a marriage work. The spiritual repercussions of divorce. What would that mean for me in the eyes of God? The impending shame of failure forced me to stay in an unfruitful marriage. The funny thing is we often pick and choose when we are concerned with God and how he will feel about us. We will justify our actions until it no longer suits us. Because if I were really concerned with God's heart for me, I would have never gotten married in the first place but I recognize that sometimes God must let you go through so he can get through for you to breakthrough!

Chapter 8
The Marriage

Nothing about our marriage was blessed. Our sex life was strained and uncomfortable. Our home life was toxic and filled with anger, frustration, and deceit. I worked like a mad person, and I can say that it was more of an escape than it was out of a financial need. Due to my inability (or so I believed) to function in a way that he thought necessary in our bedroom, he quickly placed the blame on me. He equated my issues to cheating. But how can I expect him to understand when he doesn't even understand himself? I would also find out later that my mother had told him that I would never be faithful to him because I was still sleeping with Shakayla's father. Which was almost laughable. He and I co-parented well but we were never couple material. She also failed to mention that she had destroyed any potential for that long ago, with more of her antics.

The financial highs and lows of our marriage would eventually become a source of stress and strain, the arguments became more frequent. His arrogance and narcissism prevented him from holding a job, he always wanted to skip the process and advance to the front of the line. He would demand raises after only being on a job 30 days. I did not understand it then, but he had many narcissistic tendencies. We would eventually be forced to move out of the house my father had gifted us. Keeping up with the mortgage coupled with Kenny's outright contempt for my father made it impossible to maintain. So, we would give up the house in Neptune and move back to Lakewood to an equally expensive home. That made no sense but at this point I just wanted peace in my home, so I obliged.

We both applied for a seasonal job catering for Georgian Court University. I got hired but he did not. As with most jobs there is a delay in your first paycheck. He flipped out when I did not get paid in his time and called the job. He berated and cursed my supervisor so bad I got fired. When I told him, he had no right to do that he simply said, "that's what he gets for not hiring me". This would not be the last time he cost me a job. I got him hired at my group home job as maintenance, not so much out of need but to calm his ego as he had started accusing me of cheating due to me working overnights. Again, always wanting what he had not yet earned he went off about a raise and got fired.

The biggest opportunity he ever cost me was a property management job. I had always worked multiple jobs, so I had been in the field for 7yrs. When I was offered the opportunity to work for the Wentworth Group, I was ecstatic. I would even have my own portfolio, managing 55 and over HOA's. The pay was great, and it allowed me to leave my 2nd job. He was fine at first but as I began advancing, he started finding fault with the job. As with any corporate position there are functions and events that you must attend. At each event he was always rude and would attempt to belittle my boss and coworkers. The final straw was a huge regional event held in Atlantic city, NJ. The company not only hosted the event, but they also paid for our rooms and rented me a car. There was an information session in the morning on the first day and that evening would be a banquet and award ceremony. I was to be honored as a rising star. He did not come with me but drove up later for the banquet.

By the time he arrived the ceremony was over, and we were all dancing and having a good time. The DJ played Souljah Boy and we all hit the dance floor. I was only 1 of 3 Black people in the entire region, so you can imagine what that dance floor looked like. I began trying to show one of the VP's how to do the dance and everyone just joined in. Unbeknownst to me, Kenny had been standing at the bar watching. Of course, that set him off. He was as per usual rude to everyone, and we ended up leaving and arguing. Once again, he accused me of cheating. But this time was different. Our argument was heard. When I returned to the office, my boss called me into the office and explained that he had to let me go for safety reasons. He felt that Kenny was dangerous and didn't want to chance him attacking myself or any other employees. That day I felt so defeated. I knew I had to decide. Kenny felt like the weight of the marriage was choking him and I felt like the marriage was suffocating me. I knew I needed something and so I would attempt to get back into the church.

Because there was always this nagging in my heart that was calling me back home. I needed to heal, I needed to be whole, I needed redemption. Each time I would attempt to go to church he would be against it. Our arguments had now turned into physical altercations. His drinking increased, and I just checked out. For the last two years of our marriage, we slept in separate bedrooms. I would sleep in one of the girl's rooms. We fought physically more than we ever had, I began to smoke cigarettes more and depression set in for both of us. I was sad, I was lonely, I was scared and unsure of what the future held.

We had one really big fight. It was so bad. My children were home and his nieces were sleeping over. It became violent, he picked me up by my neck and dropped me on a ceramic tile floor, this man is 6'3. That was the night I fought for my life in a way that I never had before. While we were fighting one of the girls came downstairs and turned on the vacuum cleaner to get our attention, to stop us from fighting. That was my reality check. That was when I knew that I could no longer stay in this place. That night he pulled out an old shotgun and told me that he would shoot me in my face, and I knew then that if I survived that moment that this relationship was over because I needed to live for my children. And because our God is sovereign, and He is who He is and all that He says He is, the gun jammed. We fought and he then turned the gun on himself. Of course, it didn't work. I ran around the corner to a friend's house and hid in her bushes.

Lenora would eventually find me sitting on her back porch. She knew my situation well as she was a survivor of domestic violence as well. She and I had become family over the years. I was her parents that helped me relocate to Florida. Her family had always been good to me, and she had always been like a big sister. Mom and Pop Campbell would always be a part of my village, they were a part of the team of angels God had assembled around me. Lenora encouraged me, but she also held me accountable for my complacency. When I returned home, he was gone or so I thought. I had called the police and I decided at that moment that I could not live in this manner anymore. Lo and behold he was hiding in the attic where he stayed for quite a few days only coming down when we were not home, and the house was empty. That was so unsettling.

Over the next few weeks, I began going to church at the urging of my daughter Shakayla. She and her sister had begun going to church with Lenora's daughter and her father. They had joined the praise dance team and he extended an invitation, so I accepted. He knew my situation. This enraged my husband and that Sunday as we sat in church, he called the church issuing threats. Whatever he said was enough for them to ask us to leave and they escorted us out. I've never in my life been so mortified. To be escorted out of a church because they feared for their safety. When I arrived home, he had been drinking and was ranting and raving that I was on a date at church. We argued and, in the process, he stormed off and proceeded to take my antique bible and set it on fire on the back porch. As the Bible was burning the glass patio table broke and when it shattered it stopped us from arguing long enough for us to take note of the glass hitting the ground. The glass fell into the shape of a heart. If I had never in my life heard God, I heard him in that moment. His heart was breaking for me and I needed to get back home to him.

I called my dad and 2 of my cousins and I told them what was going on and that I would need them to help me move out. It was on this day however all the years of pain and pressure had simply come to a head and S.H.E the woman that I had been suppressing for years, the girl that had endured so much, had begun to implode. You see this day was not only the end of a 10-year relationship but also the beginning of the end of the person I had allowed life to turn me into. This was me saying goodbye to a great friend but a bad husband. The reality that I had ignored for so long had finally settled in and although we entered the union with the best of intentions neither of us was prepared to be what the other needed. Two very broken people trying to heal each other without having healed themselves was for sure a recipe for disaster.

I worked for two months straight to save for the deposit on a home in freehold, a place I knew I would be safe and surrounded by family. Two months to the day my family pulled up with a U-Haul and escorted my children and I out of the home that I would share with my husband. The night before I moved out, he attempted to apologize halfheartedly; he expressed how he felt so broken, he cried, we both did but for different reasons. I had flipped the switch on my heart, and I was no longer invested in this situation.

I tried my best to express to him that I was not his forever and he was not mine. I tried to be gentle with my words and encourage him the best way I knew how while being careful not to anger him. He slept in my arms that night believing that I would stay. I lay awake knowing that I would not and the next morning when they arrived to move me out, he stayed upstairs and watched out of our bedroom window as I packed up my belongings, my children and walked out of the home we shared for the last time. I informed him that the bills were paid, and the rent was paid for the next 30 days, and he would have 30 days to find a place to stay but our marriage was over.

I was on my way to my new beginning. Once again, we started our new life, our new journey in a new town, well new to them but old to me as I was born and raised in freehold, and it was the safest place for us to be at the moment as I did not really know or understand my husband's state of mind at the time that we separated. I needed to be surrounded by family and friends to get through this and I knew that. So, I returned to my village, and they would cover me as they had always done.

Chapter 9
The Wilderness

It was not easy to leave behind a 10-year friendship and what I thought was love. Over the next few months, he would call incessantly he would curse me, send the police to my home in the middle of the night and threaten me. Eventually it began to take a toll on me, and I fell into a depression. I had come to a place where I felt that I would not be able to live in peace in New Jersey and I needed to move as far away from him as possible. So that summer I sent my children to Georgia to stay with my sister and to give me time to figure it all out. The separation was harder than I had anticipated. He had put sugar in my gas tank while I was at work so I was out of a vehicle. My finances were in disarray, and I was struggling to make ends meet in a way I had never known before.

That summer I went through many stages of highs and lows. I rebelled against the years I had spent wearing dresses down to my ankles and never wearing shorts. Not cutting my hair all out of respect for my husband. With that in mind I decided my long hair that hang down to the middle of my back, the hair he coveted had to go. I went to my good friend and had her shave it off only leaving it long on one side in an asymmetrical cut. Oh, but my rebellion did not stop there. I began to wear more form fitting clothes. I started to wear shorts. I started dating and I found myself being so cruel and cold to the men I dated oftentimes not even shielding one from the other. I would travel back and forth between New Jersey and Georgia trying to find a place and secure employment. I finally officially filed for divorce through the courts to which he responded by filing an answer suing me for alimony.

The divorce process would drag on for months because he refused to accept the papers. Meanwhile my rebellion against the 10 years that I felt I had lost continued but only proved to be more detrimental to not only my mental health but my physical health. I found myself easily fatigued and tired with constant body aches. I was sick often and I missed my children as we had never been separated. My friends had started to become worried.

One of my good friends demanded that I get out of bed, get dressed and go out with her one evening to meet someone special to her. I dragged myself out of bed throwing on the first thing I could find, which happened to be a quarter length sweater. I had lost so much weight from stress; I was able to wear it as a dress. I ran the flatiron through my hair and embarked on this outing with her, her sister and brother. I was in such a dark and lonely place then.

When we arrived at the restaurant, I sat at the bar, ordered some wings, a cosmopolitan and a slice of cheesecake. I was uncomfortable and did not want to be talked to. I had no interest in any type of social interaction. While sitting at the bar my cell phone began to ring and it was my Was-band (soon to be ex-husband) demanding to know where I was, fuming because he knew that I was out. Before I could respond my friend's sister grabbed the phone out of my hands and yelled into it for him to leave me alone and stop harassing me. She hung up but that only infuriated him more and he sent the police to my house that night. It was that night that however God's plan for my life or at least part of it would be set into motion unbeknownst to me.

See that night I was there because my friend was to meet up with someone that she had been dating and he happened to bring some friends and his brother with him. My friend and her sister however had a little too much to drink and showed out! I was Visibly uncomfortable not just because I did not want to be there but also because of their behavior. Her date's brother noticed my discomfort and how out of sorts I was. He approached me and asked if I was OK, and I rolled my eyes and told him I was fine. Now any other guy would have walked away took the hint and let me be with my wings and Cosmo, but he sat down beside me anyway despite how rude I was, he said his name was Micah and initiated a conversation and no matter how short I continued to be he kept making casual conversation. Needless to say, by the end of the evening we were having a great conversation and I even relented to dance with him. At some point he took my phone, entered his number and called himself. I had no idea that gentleman would be a catalyst in changing my life forever.

At the end of the night, he walked me to my car to ensure I got in safely. As he walked away another guy approached me and was being aggressive about getting my number. I don't know what it was but something about that moment made him turn around. He politely nudged the other guy out of the way, which I found amusing. We exchanged a few words and he gently kissed me on the cheek smiled and walked away. I rolled my eyes and thought the nerve of this negro, who does he think he is. He tried it. As my friend, her sister and brother all loaded up into the car, I asked her who he was, and she explained that it was her date's brother. We giggled about it on the way home until they fell asleep. I drove because I was the sober one.

It would be two weeks before I heard anything from Micah which was fine by me because I had no intentions on calling him. We met April 17th, 2010, and two weeks to the day my phone rang, and I would hear this deep but gentle voice on the other end asking how I was and if I remembered him. Of course, I did but I pretended not to. we ended up having about a 2-hour conversation. He was easy to talk to and he kept me laughing. From that day on we would talk on the phone daily at length about any and everything and although I was still very broken and hurting something about him made me want to get to know him something about him wanted me to let him know me. Not the me the world had come to know, but the me I kept for me. There was nothing superficial about our conversations. He became my therapist. Make no mistake the past was still controlling me, and I kept him at a healthy distance. During this time, I went and picked up my children from Georgia and brought them home just to spend some time with them.

I missed them dearly and still very much battling depression, I would lay in the bed only getting up to ensure that they ate and to go to work. My youngest at the time had started to go to church. My home church where my maternal grandmother attended happened to be right around the corner from our house so when she got up on Sunday mornings and walked to church, I assumed that was where she was going. One Sunday she came into my room profoundly serious and explained to me that I needed to get up. She pleaded with me to get out of the bed and explained that she did not want me to die, that she was afraid for me.

This brought me to heal quickly, and the tears welled up in my eyes. I knew that I had to get up so that I would not stay in this mental space. So, I got up, got dressed and went to church with Shakayla leading the way. I pulled around the corner and went to pull into my home church. She stopped me and said no this is not where we are going, go that way. I followed her instructions and asked her curiously where we are going. She said I have been going to New Hope. I have not been going to great grandma's church. I have been going to this church, she pointed as we pulled into the parking lot. I continued to follow her lead into the church. We found a seat in the back corner. I sat still and listened to this voice loud and bustling.

The voice of Pastor Vester Dock, a pastor full of energy delivering a sermon that felt like it was just for me. I never opened my mouth. I just cried, Evangelist Edgerton came and sat next to me, wrapped her arm around me and gently wiped my tears. She never said a word or asked a question and from that Sunday to the next four Sundays I would go to that church, sit in the corner and cry silently and she would do it all over again. My silent rumblings, my cries to the Heavenly Father however were not as silent as I thought. Those around me could feel the measures of my pain.

After 30 days of crying and praying, the 1st Sunday of the new month came. I sat through the service and I cried as I had done for the month prior but at the end of this service as I went to leave Pastor Dock stopped me and said I want to talk to you. I was a little thrown off because I was a stranger to him and was confused as to what he would want to speak to me about. I agreed and Evangelist Edgerton joined us. Once in his office we sat down and he said "I allowed you time, I allowed you time to cry, I allowed you time but now you need to tell me what is going on so that I can help you, those tears, your tears require some help and healing. I saw your daughter bring you here. That baby recognizes that you need help, I can't let you leave here the way you came. If you would let us, we want to help you." I opened my mouth and began to tell my story.

I held nothing back. Evangelist Edgerton sat next to me and held my hand while I told my story. When I finished, he prayed with me, prayed for me and he promised that he would always be available to me and that he was going to help me because I needed to heal. He assured me that he recognized the God in me, but he was also sure to give me correction and say that I had gotten in my own way that my suffering was partly my own doing as I was not obedient to the things that I knew God wanted for me. A harsh but true reality I thought and from that day forward each Sunday that I attended church he and I would talk and pray, and Evangelists Edgerton would talk and pray with me, and she would check on me often. I had begun my journey to healing.

In the meantime, with my children back in Georgia by June my relationship with Micah had begun to take on a deeper meaning and he had become an integral part in my healing. He would encourage me when I was down, he would remind me daily that I was beautiful, he would remind me daily that I was worth it and worthy of love, but he would also give me just the right amount of accountability for my part in the things that I felt were wrong in my life. I still held him at a distance but would look forward to our lengthy conversations. Between his friendship and my realignment with God, my healing process was well underway.

One of the many things I credit Micah with is teaching and guiding me through the process of becoming comfortable in my sexuality. As a sexual abuse survivor, my ability to truly engage in and enjoy sexual encounters was severely inhibited. Combined with the way females are taught from a young age modesty, and it is drilled into our heads to refrain from sex and pregnancy is used as a threat as well as our reputation. These things had crippled me, hindered my ability to function in sexual relationships. I was uncomfortable with my own body and ignorant to its most basic functions. Most women do not even understand what they are feeling while having sex. It could take years before some even grasp the concept of an orgasm. Something I would soon discover. In contrast boys are celebrated for their conquest and sexual development.

Micah listened intently when I spoke and was always careful to meet me where I was at that moment. He encouraged me to look at myself in the mirror and become familiar with my body and how it functioned. He was fully invested in building me up in all areas of my life, he was invested in loving me to wholeness and I was oblivious. He walked me through each step of discovering myself. I followed his instructions reluctantly and all though I was alone there was still an air of shame that lingered in the room. It would take me months to work through just the first layer of my issues in that area and years to overcome it all together.

I can say that 11 years after meeting the one God kept for me, I am finally operating from a place of wholeness. I have become comfortable and confident in my sexuality. I now know and understand my love language and can make my needs known. What a love. Now my ex-husband had finally stop calling or at least not calling as often and I was finally getting some balance and gaining my footing being a single woman again but the God we serve always has a greater plan than anything we could imagine.

Chapter 10
A New Beginning

Micah and I did not go on our first official date until August 2010. It was a simple date to play miniature golf and then out for ice cream. After our first date we continued to talk and began spending more and more time with one another, me still being cautious and sticking with my plan to move to Georgia. but God I had found a home in Georgia and was on my way. Micah and I talked the entire drive there and he would be gracious enough to pack up my entire house and store my things. We would sit on the phone and talk all day and all night. It did however come as a surprise when he eventually said I am going to relocate. I'm coming to join you in Georgia. I was in shock. I thought he was nuts. I was afraid I was nervous but there was something about him and love had truly started to bloom.

I was still very much working on myself and trying to be the best healthy me I could be and not just for my children this time but for me because I recognized that I needed to free me from the ties that bind by this point. I realized that I needed to pray and break some generational curses, that I needed to free myself of some words that were spoken over my life as a child and in order for me to truly have healing and be my best self that had to be our priority.

The beauty in him was that he was willing to wait, he was willing to walk me through the process, he was willing to hold my hand and wipe my tears as I wrestled with my healing. He was willing to move at my pace and to wait for me. So, when he could not get a transfer, I made the decision to come back. I brought my children back to New Jersey because something about this man, something about this man made me feel certain, assured, and strong with him, I was capable. So, I came back to New Jersey and decided to build a life here and see where this new thing would go. Only having been gone a little over a month by November I was back in New Jersey and exploring this new relationship. When God has his hand on something and it is for you, he will remove every obstacle and clear a path for you to receive your blessing and he did.

My divorce was finalized in January of 2011, I sat in that courtroom alone, my ex-husband did not even bother to show up. As the judge read the decree out loud, I was bombarded by a flood of fleeting emotions. The tears crept from my eyes as the reality set in that this chapter of my life was now complete. As I walked out of the courtroom with each step, I felt lighter and by the time I made it to the door I left the past right there! On the courthouse floor. I got in the car and drove off with a renewed purpose, I was driving into my new beginning and new it would be.

I got a call from my maternal grandmother that she wanted to come for a visit from North Carolina. By this time Micah and I had found a place of our own and were expecting our first child. We drove down and picked her up and she came to stay with us under the guise that she wanted to see everyone for Mother's Day. Crafty old lady that she was, had a plan that she and Micah had concocted.

Micah and I had talked about marriage but made no concrete plans. It was a normal day for me. I went to shower and when I went to step out, there this man was on one knee holding a ring. Lord have mercy. What in the world was he thinking? Here I am just out of the shower, like dude you could not let me get cute? Sheesh. That is who he is. Genuine, spontaneous, and loving. I said yes and when I walked out of the bathroom, I walked right into my father in-law. I investigated my living room, and it was full of people and my grandmother was grinning from ear to ear. You see Micah had gotten her blessing and I had been had by the best to ever do it. My grandmother Betty Mae.

So, with my grandmother's blessing Micah and I got married that day May 3rd, 2010. One year and three weeks after our first meeting. We would also welcome our first child October 16th, 2011. I would never have thought that this type of love could be possible. I had never taken birth control during my first marriage and one of our many issues was infertility. Now here I was with a brand-new love and baby. Like Hannah God had closed my womb for a season and in his sovereign time he opened it. Just like that. God was truly doing what he does best bringing his divine order to my life.

Our journey was not an easy one as I was still very much broken but as I would learn later, I was beautifully broken. My healing process would take years. Our marriage would be tested repeatedly as would my patience. Micah did not come without a price. That price would come in the form of my bonus baby and that currency brought with her a mother. As with most blended families, we were rarely short on the drama. Whenever amicable resolutions cannot be obtained privately, the next step is usually the courts. She chose the courts, and this affected my husband's ability to be a father and effectively coparent.

To go from having full access to his child to now being told when, where and how he could love her almost broke him. I was not spared either. My character was frequently attacked. I was used as the catalyst for her outburst. I was blamed for her crusade to separate him from his child. Because although they were not in a relationship when he and I started dating, he had always allowed her full access to him and now that access was denied. In the beginning it was hurtful. To be used as the weapon to hurt my husband in that way almost tore me apart. At one point I considered letting him go. I knew and understood what it was like to be used as a weapon against a parent. The hurt and sense of loss it created in me was not something I wanted to be a party to creating in that child. I sought God for an answer. He made it clear to me that unfortunately it didn't matter who Micah chose this would always be the result. These issues truly had nothing to do with me and everything to do with her and her inability to acknowledge and accept responsibility for the decisions she had made concerning their relationship.

Accountability is a key component to anyone's healing journey. Without it how can a corrective course of action ever take place? God assured me that this was not my burden to bear. So, we moved forward with the blessing that mattered most. God's blessing.

Eventually he and I learned to just accept the situation for what it was. We knew in our hearts that we had done nothing to deserve her anger. We understood that she had healing of her own to do and so we agreed to leave her in God's hands and hope that one day she would see the error in her actions and find healing. It was one of the hardest seasons in our marriage. I had to watch and pray as my husband grieved the loss of his child's presence in his life. Over the years we would spend more time in court than he did with his child. With each new court date leaving him more and more defeated and our only recourse was prayer.

He decided that it was doing the child more harm than good to keep going in and out of court. He stopped attending and once again left it in God's hands. The best place for it.

He was also human and had lived a life before me that had left many wounds, he needed to heal from that we would discover sooner than later. Over the years our relationship would take many twists and turns but with each new turn this man would stand firm by my side holding my hand wiping my tears praying with me, praying over me, praying for me and he would be invested in my healing and growth. I would then take each new skill I learned from him and use it to help him heal.

As I was still going through the process of detaching myself from the toxic parts of my mother and learning to love myself, my journey would only prove to be more challenging as I got closer to this goal. As with everything new and good thing in my life my mother tried her hardest to break us even going as far as to tell him that I would never be faithful to him. At one point against his better judgment, we allowed her to move into our home for a short time and the level of disregard and disrespect that she displayed towards my marriage, towards my husband and my children was so hurtful that I had to physically remove her from our home.

She tried to attack him physically. You see unlike my first marriage Micah saw her for who and what she was and refused to bow down to her tirades or allow her to berate and disrespect me in his presence. This made her despise him more, but this man would not grow weary. He stood firm and continued to cover me and protect me on my path to healing. It takes a strong man to love a broken woman. To hold her hand and lift her head as she's going and growing through. It is not an assignment for the faint at heart and my husband has shown time and time again that he was in fact made for such a time as this. I pray that God continues to reward his tenacity and faithfulness.

God has a funny way of showing up when you least expect it and when I look back over my life I can recall and recount countless times that he has shown up for me when I did not even realize he was showing up for me. He knew that for me to get to where I needed to be, he would have to create a great divide between the toxicity that lived in my mother and me. He also knew that I would need someone to support and love me through those rough moments someone who would encourage support and push me when I was not strong enough to encourage and push myself. God knew that my children would need someone to maintain the structure and safety they required while I was going through my moment.

Yes, I can equate my struggles to a moment because now they seem so far away, and they are not as big in the grand scheme of my life. I can now say with certainty that I was safe in God's arms all along and that he had covered me when I could not cover myself. Although I have suffered some hardships and some devastating losses, he worked it all out for my good and it will serve me well as I pick up the mantle and walk in the calling that is on my life.

Chapter 11
Answering The Call

In order to be a true leader, you have to know what it means to suffer and serve. You must know empathy and understand that there is a difference between that and sympathy. You must be resilient, reliable and you must have a heart for the people that God is going to assign you to. These are all things that my maternal grandmother knew when she spoke these fateful words over my life when I was three years old and many more times over the years. She told me that there was a calling on my life and that my connection to God was bigger than anything that I would ever know or understand, she would also issue many stern warnings to me about my behavior and how it would end if I did not get some "act right" as she called it. In those moments, I received it as a child. Not fully understanding the magnitude of what was to come. I did not understand that for every trial and tribulation that I would suffer or go through my reward would be much greater in Christ.

Through my healing and ever evolving relationship with God, I am learning to rely on him more. To trust him in those moments where I don't have all the answers and even those where I think I do. My prayer life has become a great source of relief, a space and time where I talk to him and patiently await his answer. Although trials and tribulations still come, I can make my way through them much easier than in previous times. I am now able to discern between the times where God was carrying me through and teaching me and those moments where the enemy was trying to keep me from my destiny even if it meant taking my life. With the support of my husband and children, I was able to complete a nursing program and am now a nurse. I chose to embrace my calling and was well on my way to manifesting all that God had promised. Oh, but the God we serve is always demanding more of us than we do of ourselves. So, he was not finished with me yet!

My husband and I had finally found our cohesive rhythm for our lives or so we thought. We have since graduated from simple struggles and just like any new level in life we now face new devils so to speak. Our trials and tribulations now contain spiritual Struggles and warfare. That's not to say that over the years my mother wouldn't continue to try to come in between us and speak ill over our marriage. We have persevered. As I grew in the church and developed a deeper relationship with God my discernment grew, and my spiritual prowess became greater. I was able to truly separate myself from the years of toxic behavior that my mother embodied. I dove headfirst into supporting my community and being the person that I needed when I was a child.

Over the summer of 2011, we also received a blessing that is our son but he did not come alone we also inherited his two sisters who for a short time resided with us. So here we are this brand-new marriage that already came with three children. We inherited a child and then I gave birth to another in October. I was not sure if it was overflow or madness. Somehow, we adjusted to our newfound family and managed to move forward building a life and our spirituality together. We found that not only did I have healing to do but he did as well. Because our foundation was built on the right things and our union was

God ordained, we found it easy to hold on to one another and support each other through our healing processes and although today the healing process continues each day it has gotten easier to love each other through the low moments just as we love each other in the high ones.

It was about the second year of our marriage that the calling became so great on my life that I could no longer ignore what God was calling me to do. Unable to ignore God's small still voice I reached out to my father who was also taking his own walk and expressed to him how I was feeling and what I was hearing from God. He began to sow into me spiritually and supply me with reading and study materials to help guide my mind in the direction it needed to go. It's funny because he was not surprised and made clear that he too was aware of the call on my life. It's amazing to finally find out how people really see you as opposed to how you think they see you. Even if they were one of your harshest critics. Even how they still see you. What they see could be the very reason they treat you so harshly or what you perceive as harsh.

My father would connect me to a childhood acquaintance who was also walking in her own spiritual elevation. I reached out to her and after explaining my situation we set a time to get together. She and I had lunch. This divine connection would help me on my journey into the next level of my calling. Now I tried to do things in decency and order and reached out to my pastor and assistant pastor to share with them my feelings and what I was going through. What I realized is when you are new in Christ and that fire is blazing inside of you, your patience is a virtue. The excitement combined with that fresh anointing can sometimes make you want to run to the finish line or what you think is the finish line until you realize that there will always be another level of learning, another level of training for you to forge ahead in your ministry. Understanding that God never stops fortifying or qualifying you for your assignment if he called you. When you begin to walk in a new calling you can sometimes overlook that the enemy is always looking for a way to distract you and in comes one of the many new devils I would face.

The more I dedicated myself to being of service the more frenemies I would acquire. In my experience "Church folk" as I call them, will pounce on the opportunity to demean babes in Christ. Especially one with promise. It's a sad reality that they are often intimidated by anything new. Where they should embrace and guide the next generation, they hold them back afraid of change and to secure what they feel is their spot. This is the cause of so many broken souls running from the church. Gone are the days of it being a safe haven. A place where being broken and damaged was acceptable because it is a place of healing. The fiber of the church has become infested with social climbing, grandstanding and a battle of the generations.

The old guard should be welcoming the new if not the church will die with them. These situations would ultimately drive a wedge between my pastor and I. Gossip and bitterness would separate us. I felt like my leaders were not receptive or did not believe in the call that was on my life, so I separated myself from them and clung strictly to my mentor. This was wrong and a clear example of how old habits die hard.

I forged ahead in developing my ministry. It would be a few years before I realized that this was a trick of the enemy to make me doubt myself and to make me doubt my calling. To doubt what God has for me. What I was missing was that even the strongest spiritual being has weak moments and can operate outside of their calling. Leaders are not exempt from spiritual warfare. This is made evident in 2nd Corinthians 12:7-10. God allowed and left Paul to do battle, he would always recognize God as his strength. Hence why it is so important to pray without ceasing and cover each other, especially our leaders.

I dove headfirst into my studies and served my mentor whenever she would go to speaking engagements to learn how to be an intercessor and how to be an adjutant because what I did know and understand was that these were skills that shape a great leader. I never officially left my church because God never told me to move. I would just take leave. I had become overwhelmed with the constant attacks on my character and not for nothing I was a bit of a hot head. I was very defensive and the enemy would take every opportunity available to use this against me. It had gotten so intense that I removed myself from anything I felt would give them a reason to say anything. If I wasn't involved, then they had no reason to come at me.

Unfortunately, it did not change a thing. These increased occurrences would serve to push me further away and out the door. How could I sit amongst these people and be ok with this behavior? The real question was how could I not but that lesson would eventually come. My husband would go on to be ordained to be a deacon and I by default as his wife. This elevation only gave them something else to antagonize me for. I was verbally attacked for wearing dress pants to serve communion. Everything I would post on my social media was scrutinized and being reported back to the pastor. It was as if the more I pulled back the more they looked for. I kept one foot out the door. The only thing keeping me there was my husband. I didn't want to leave him to fight alone. He was dealing with his own struggles. So, I held on as best I could.

In my mind how could I sit under someone who allowed so much to go on, that allowed me to suffer such cruelty at the hands of other members. Yet again another trick of the enemy. It was not that he was allowing it. He understood fully what the call on my life was. He understood fully where God was trying to elevate me too and for years, he would call my name and tell me to make sure I "got right". He understood that if I couldn't deal with people being cold to me or mean to me or lying on me or talking about me that I could not be an effective leader because these things will come and I would need to know how to love in spite of, that I would need to understand that the very people that would be kicking me, talking about me, lying on me and belittling me would be the very people that God would expect for me to serve, to pray over, to pray with, to teach and to sow into. Hence why he allowed me to go through these things so that I could become the leader he knows and knew that I could be. He was also a man with his own warfare to contend with. I had to learn to be slow to anger and quick to pray.

Chapter 12
Forgiveness

Now over the years my maternal grandmother and I would find ourselves worlds apart. Differences of opinion on family matters and our shared stubborn nature put a strain on our relationship. Not to mention the deep-rooted resentment I had developed over the years due to my childhood. I knew my grandmother loved me but had grown to resent her for sugar coating so much of my mother's bad behavior. When her health started to fail in June 2016, I did not miss a beat stepping up to care for her. During those months leading up to her death, we spoke at length about a lot of things. I gained a greater understanding of the woman I called grandma. We forgave each other and she found it in her heart to apologize for her part in my suffering. She also asked that I forgive my mother, really forgive her. She also instructed me to look after my aunts and uncles. I couldn't believe my ears. I had finally earned her respect, but she let me know that she always knew who I was destined to be. She would also trust me with her final arrangements.

On November 26th, 2016, laying in a hospital bed She asked for her sisters. I made the necessary calls to gather everyone she requested. That included the Aunt I had lived with years ago as a teenager. She was away in Africa and I was forced to reach out to her husband to contact her. I sent a short message informing him of the situation. He attempted to respond with small talk. I ignored his messages and blocked him.

By the 29th all her sisters had arrived. I had honored her request. After they left, I lay my head on the bed next to her and cried. I cried for all the time lost, I cried because she was the link to so many experiences in my life. I cried because her acknowledgment and apology had given me a freedom, I did not know I needed. She had unlocked the shackles of a portion of my past that had me bound for years. As I lay there, she touched my head and whispered I am going home. I sobbed harder. She told me to hush she was still here. When visiting hours were over, I told her I loved her, and I forgave my mother. I left. When I arrived the next morning, she had done exactly what she said she would do. She had gone home, to sit at the feet of the father. She had spent the last few months making things right with me. She also changed the narrative on how the family was to view me by leaving me "in charge" of her final wishes. I was her granddaughter and she loved me. As for my aunt. Well, she and I remained cordial, but she not once acknowledged what had transpired while I was in her care. I honestly didn't expect her to. When she left, I did hug her and whispered I forgive you. She looked down, grabbed her suitcase, and walked toward the elevator to leave.

We buried my grandmother December 9th, by December 11th my mother would be in a coma. I believe my grandmother knew this was coming and she knew I would need to be there to pray my mother through. Pray is exactly what I did. My mother would come out of the coma but her health would never be the same. She was in stage 4 heart failure. I would once again become her caregiver. It was different this time because I truly forgave her and was moving in love and not childish adoration.

Forgiving her freed me, not her. She will have to answer for her wrongs just not to me. I am ok with that. I realized the anger and hurt I was carrying was not weighing her down but hindering me. I also learned that because I was holding on to all of that she was still in control. By forgiving her completely, I took my life back. I was no longer at the mercy of her emotions. I was free and available to the will of God. I was so bound by anger; I could not freely serve God because I was a slave to my emotions. It was time to level up.

Chapter 13
Redemption

Under the guidance and encouragement of my mentor I took the leap and began accepting speaking assignments. One assignment in particular stands out to me. God would take me to a book in the bible that I had always steered clear of. Revelations 12:6 The woman in the wilderness. After reading and studying extensively I became intrigued by this woman. I began to see so much of myself in this woman. Her crown was the weight of my calling, the moon under her feet was my past, the dragon was all the trauma of my past and some from my present, the things the enemy was chasing me with to stop my birthing process and the baby was my gifts, my calling. Like the woman God would eventually align me with a wilderness to cover me. My "wilderness" would come in the form of 4 women. My sisters. The Mighty 7.

By the 5th year of my spiritual evolution, God started giving me visions of a women's ministry. This came as no surprise. I had always served women and children and one area that was very important to me was creating support systems for women amongst women. I realized if my mother had had a stronger support system, sisters to check her and check in on her. Her life may have been different. After much travailing I finally broke down and was obedient to God. I moved forward with creating the women's ministry S.H.E Changes Everything. S.H.E was an acronym for Saved Healed Enough. This was personal to me because I needed to know and understand that I was in fact Saved Healed and Enough. I needed to know and understand that God knew my name no matter what was being said about me in the world, it was what he called me in the spirit that truly mattered. S.H.E changes everything, S.H.E is me, it was never about the people around me and how they felt about me nor the things that they had spoken over and into my life, but it was always about me and how I felt about me and what I knew to be true.

God wanted me to know that S.H.E is me and that no matter what obstacle had come my way you have managed to push through and persevere. You are a daughter of the Most High God. A daughter of the king and under God's banner I am saved I am healed, and I am enough. My grandmother used to say it's not what you are called it's what you answer to. I no longer answer to any other name than the one God calls me by. The derogatory names that people called me I no longer associate myself with, I am not my parent's failures, their trials, or their tribulations because those things were theirs and theirs alone. Even in poor health my mother's toxic behavior will still show itself but I no longer answer to it. I know whose I am and who I am. I am not their tragedy, but God I am his Victory.

I know and understand that each person born on this earth has their own path that God has carved out for them. The father knew us before we were formed in our mothers' wombs and designed our calling. His designs and desires for us are based on individuality not uniformity. I know and I understand that the God I serve never left me and his desire for me was not to die but to live, to win, but like all things I would have to earn that win. By the 6th year in February of 2019, I would finally step out of the shadows and into the light of my destiny with the official launch of S.H.E Changes Everything. I would step out with my very first event. It was to be a vision board workshop and brunch that included fellowship and a good word from 6 other Woman of God that the father had placed in my spirit and aligned me with. I had been introduced to some and reintroduced to others over time. He was designing the Mighty 7.

So, when I asked God how I was to bring this program together. He placed this amazing strong group of women in my spirit to help me launch the vision. What I would later come to realize is that during each passing year and each new program not only would we be sowing into the people; we would be sowing into each other. It would be as much for us as it was for those that we were serving. From walking in our purpose to realizing the vision and now becoming the vision God used my journey to help other women who were also going through the process that I was going through. And through this ministry I would gain a sisterhood rooted in love, friendship accountability encouragement and acceptance. It would change my life forever. Through these newfound relationships and God ordained connections I have begun my journey to fully embracing my calling and coming out of the shadows to being a better Me. Unfortunately, incoming......new devil loading.

Chapter 14
Flawed but Favored

Of course, the enemy would not just allow me to step into my destiny seamlessly. He is after all the author of confusion. Almost immediately "church folk" would find fault in and create issues where there were none. Carnal minded people tend to formulate their own theories instead of asking for clarity. One of the misconceptions was that M7 was simply a circle to join. It was not. It wasn't even something we created or were prepared for. I saw the 6 ladies God chose as simply speakers, but we know God always has a greater purpose for us. It was revealed to us at the close of the first S.H.E event that there was in fact a corporate ministry to be birthed out of that pairing.

We decided in our post conference that we were willing to accept whatever it was God required of us. We spent 1 year praying and strategizing on how we could be effective and build this ministry. Our prayer was for God to show us what it was he required of us and how he wanted us to achieve it. Because what we did understand was that although birthed through the S.H.E platform, the assignment for the S.H.E ministry was a separate assignment than that of M7 and in order to be affective we would have to be as specific in the prayer and planning for M7 as we were for our individual ministries.

While we were being obedient to God the enemy would be campaigning against us before we could even get started. One person in particular felt left out. She didn't understand and never bothered to ask what the next steps were going to be. She didn't understand that we first needed to develop a true authentic sisterhood before we could minister to others and be used to foster divine connections between others. We needed to be able to speak to with absolution what sisterhood really entailed. The good, the bad and the ugly. Because understanding was never sought it became a smear campaign against M7.

The poison would eventually make its way into the pulpit of my church. I was so taken aback to hear a pastor speak the words that "we" had somehow made her feel like she was less than! That was just so out of line to me. Once again, I would take 2 steps backward and neglect my own ministry to focus on protecting the image of the one birthed through me. God did eventually settle it in my spirit that until a person is willing to see themselves and own their own feelings, they will never be able to see anyone else's. I would have to just leave her in God's hands. God didn't stop there. One of my greatest tests would push me to a broken and almost irreparable place. Just as I was walking into a place of security, I had finally gained my footing and was at the pinnacle of my healing process God would once again bring correction and test my faith.

During all the chaos I had become so dependent on the validation of others that I had stopped seeking the validation of the father. Those I had deemed "accomplished" in my mind; I began to take their word as "gospel" so to speak. I had become so consumed with meeting the needs of others that I had neglected to meet my own. Due to all the negative noise blaring around me, I clung to the constant reassurance I was receiving from others. In an effort to maintain these positive affirmations, I slipped back into people pleasing. I dedicated myself to proving that I was not what the world said I was. Those old toxic habits had started to resurface but the father said no you have come too far to go backwards. So, God did what he did best and allowed for a separation and severance of those soul ties.

A common misconception is that soul ties are formed through physical contact alone. This is a misguided notion. Soul ties can also be formed where there is a strong influence over and in your life. Yes, soul ties can result from friendships or any close relationship with unhealthy boundaries. Over time a deep bond or tie can be formed. For me I was in such a vulnerable place in my spirituality and healing from so many traumatic experiences it was easy for me to fall victim to my own mind. In layman's terms I had developed "hero" syndrome. Because I still had a skewed view of myself, I had come to believe that my purpose was only to sow into and build up others. I had become comfortable being in the background and in doing so placed people on pedestals they didn't ask to be on.

I grieved this situation almost like a death, because for me it was. Something had to die in order for me to live. The break in these relationships although devastating had to happen. The father reassured me that although it may not feel like it now, this is simply a season of realignment between him and I. You see I had become so comfortable standing behind that I was almost afraid to step up and out. I had become complacent. We often get so comfortable in the routine of doing things that it is hard for us to come out of our comfort zone. The God that we serve has a way of making us quite uncomfortable when he wants and demands change. He knew and understood that if he did not create some level of separation between those relationships and myself that I would not ever truly step out, step up and begin to operate fully in my calling. The father knew that I had become so comfortable and codependent on their sheer presence that my dependence on him had dwindled but the God we serve is a jealous God and will not share our adoration on that level.

During this season God would also take the time to teach me a valuable lesson in forgiveness and adjust my posture so I would begin to walk in love. Ephesians 5:1-2 states ``Be ye therefore followers of God, as dear children; 2. And walk in love, as Christ also hath loved us, and hath given himself for us an offering and sacrifice to God for a sweet-smelling savor." God requires that in all things we walk in love. And in order to walk in love we must embody a forgiving spirit and heart. Because how could I serve God's people and be unable to forgive? How could I teach forgiveness if I don't know how to forgive? Forgiveness is one of God's greatest teachings aside from love. Unforgiveness is a symptom of being wounded and being wounded means you are carrying hurt and unattended hurt will hinder you from healing. You cannot teach God's people what you don't know, what you have never experienced. Your experiences are what help shape the type of leader you will be.

This separation that God had orchestrated was also a multi-faceted lesson. One of the many lessons I have had to learn on this journey that is life. One thing I took away from this situation is that our innate desire for acceptance and validation can hinder us in our growth process. We can become so enthralled with wanting others to recognize the very things that we should see in ourselves! Learning to accept these things and be OK if others don't recognize them. God recognized that this was not the first time that these traits had surfaced and that they reflected my childhood desires for the validation of people I viewed as authoritative figures. God knew that I needed to take those childhood traumas and rip them out by the root and although I had made progress there was still work to be done for me to be my best self.

God knew I had finally learned and accepted that he had the final say that he and he alone had called me by name to pick up a mantle that was left behind by my grandmother. God needed me to see and understand that it was a mantle that I could not transfer or ignore and in order to do that he needed to take away my safety net. He forced me to stand on him and him alone. He knew it would not be easy, so he created divine connections to walk me into the next season of my journey. He also made clear to me that our story had not stopped there and in due season he would teach me the lesson of restoration. Our God is strategic in that way as he also assured me that they too required this separation to move forward in what he had called them to do.

Although it looked as if they were where God had intended them to be, I was reminded that just because it looks well put together does not mean the stitching is firm. There was still work to be done and more birthing for them to do.

We must know and understand that every relationship we walk in may not be meant for a lifetime. Some people are only meant to accompany you through a season and in God's time all season's transition into new seasons or come to an end. We must also be aware that just as we are ever evolving, those we may be assigned to or are assigned to us are also ever evolving. We must allow room for them to grow as we expect them to make room for our growth and if that growth shifts them away from you, don't take it personal. Count it all joy and know and understand that God does all things well and for our good. Including shifting people around so that he gets the glory, and the assignment can be completed. No person or thing is ours to keep. Each and every one of us belongs to God and God alone. Take the lesson from the relationship and keep your eyes on God. If it's meant to be God will orchestrate restoration in his time. He's NEVER lost a battle and does all things well.

So, although what I thought was a loss of relationship hurt me deeply, I have matured enough spiritually to accept what I cannot change because I am not the author nor finisher of my life. I now know and understand that the shift was meant for our good and was necessary, When the hurt feelings subsided and grief past, The love remained, and it will forever! Frick and Frack had to evolve, the women with hope had to emerge!

Throughout my life like a chameleon, I learned to adapt to my surroundings. As I adapted, I added another layer over my previous environment. The weight of those different personas became heavy and made me weak. Weak spiritually and weak physically. Mental and spiritual warfare if left to fester will begin to manifest in physical ways. So as God forced me to see myself, sit with myself. I was able to gain a better perspective of who it is I am truly meant to be and actually want to be. I realized that I have triggers and due to the level of my childhood trauma I was suffering from PTSD. Through prayer and fasting, I was able to center myself. I also began to make decisions with my best interest in mind.

I now know and understand that I placed people in a position to disappoint me. They did not ask to be placed on the pedestals I placed them on in my mind's eye and just like me they are human. I cannot hold them to a standard I don't want to be held to. What I can do is set boundaries for how I want to be treated and what I will and will not accept. I had to learn the value that has always lived in me. Now that I know and understand these basic principles, people no longer have the power to invoke a reaction I do not want to provide. I will still have moments of weakness as I am human and deliverance takes time. I now know and fully understand the beauty in being me. That there is not one thing that I have survived that God has not sanctioned and brought me through.

Just like my story does not look like anyone else's my ministry will not either. God made clear that he qualified me with every new trial and tribulation. My life was quite messy, tangled and tumultuous but God I survived. I survived so that God could use me to save someone else. God chose me because I had nothing to lose but everything to gain. Just like Elijah I had been suicidal, like Joseph I had suffered abuse, like Gideon I operated in fear, like Jonah I ran, like The Samaritan woman I was divorced and like Peter I used foul language and denied God but the most important commonality between us is God still found me worthy. Jesus used the flawed and broken to serve the flawed and broken.

The first step for me was seeing me as I am. Now that I see me, I also know and recognize unhealthy behaviors, because they don't work for my good but against it. My traumas are now my triumphs and testimony. Someone will be saved somewhere because I travailed, fought and lived. Although my journey is still in progress, when I look back at how far I have come, I am in awe of all that I have survived. I am reminded daily with blessed assurance that the father does all things well and that includes me! I started off this new year launching all that I have been holding on to. I am finally becoming the Vision that he gave me some years ago. I stepped into this new season of my life with a newfound confidence, a stronger sense of security and renewed spiritual prowess. I have learned that although salvation is a choice, an acceptance of God's love for you, and willingness to submit to the will of the father.

Deliverance is a journey. A long tedious journey. Because we wrestle with our flesh and sin daily. Deliverance takes time, it encompasses our healing and ability to step outside of ourselves and see us. It requires us to self-evaluate and be conscious of our shortcomings. It's constantly asking God for forgiveness, protection and guidance. These things will not only build a greater relationship between you and him, but they will also help you build character. Do not be afraid of your mess. Life is messy, that is the beauty in serving a sovereign God. He knows and understands.

He loves us in spite of. Yes, you will encounter naysayers, not everyone will be receptive to your gifts but if God called you, he qualified you to be of service for someone. Once I understood these things, I came to have a greater sense of purpose and am evolving into the true manifestation of the woman God has called me to be. So, I encourage you today to step up and step out on faith.

Embrace your calling and walk in your purpose, on purpose, with purpose. S.H.E has emerged, the manifestation has begun and S.H.E is YOU and ME! Launch the Vision Sis. God's Grace is sufficient.

Stay tuned the best is yet to come!!!

Meet The Author

Thank you for reading my story. My goal is to inspire you to start your own journey of healing to wholeness by sharing this candid account of my life's experiences. If you haven't already be sure to get your copy of the accompanying interactive journal to help guide you along the way. I pray this book inspires and encourages you.

Chalmar G. Ramey

www.savedhealedenough.com

You can continue follow my journey by subscribing to my Youtube channel S.H.E Emerged or listening to my podcast S.H.E Emerged on Apple. Spotify, iheart radio, or google podcast

Scan with your phones camera